No Sin in Paradise

No Sin in Paradise

Dijorn Moss

www.urbanchristianonline.com

Urban Books, LLC
97 N18th Street
Wyandanch, NY 11798

ISBN 13: 978-1-60162-677-6
ISBN 10: 1-60162-677-0

First Trade Paperback Printing September 2014
Printed in the United States of America

10 9 8 7 6 5 4 3 2 1

Distributed by Kensington Corp.
Submit Wholesale Orders to:
Kensington Publishing Corp.
C/O Penguin Group (USA) Inc.
Attention: Order Processing
405 Murray Hill Parkway
East Rutherford, NJ 07073-2316
Phone: 1-800-526-0275
Fax: 1-800-227-9604

Dedication

To my granny Ruth Jonice
"The Queen of Queens."

To my muse Trinea Moss
I love you just as Christ loves the church.

To my son Caleb
My greatest joy is watching you grow up.

Acknowledgments

I would not have completed this book if it were not for my Lord and Savior Jesus Christ. I am reminded every day that I am fulfilling your purpose for my life. Since becoming a parent, I have developed a profound appreciation for my parents. To my mother and father, thank you for molding me into the man that I am today. To my family and close friends, thank you for your love and continued support over the years.

To my editor Joy, thank you for constantly pushing me to deliver my best and challenging me to become a better writer. I truly thank God for both your faith and your wisdom. You deserve all of your success, and then some.

On this extraordinary journey, God has blessed me to be taught by some of the greatest minds the earth has ever produced. One of those mentors is Minister Kevin Murray. The Lord has called him home, but his legacy and his words remain. One of his greatest sermons was about pressing toward the mark and not letting the fog set in and cloud your vision. I am thankful for Pastor Dace and Bible Way Christian Center. My life has been enriched as a result of your ministry. To Bishop Noel Jones and City of Refuge, thank you for warmth and your kindness. Finally, to Pastor Bayless Conely and Cottonwood Church, thank you for being a great spiritual home.

I also would like to acknowledge the writers who inspired me and have inspired Nicodemus Dungy: Walter Mosley, Michael Connelly, and the late Elmore Leonard.

Acknowledgments

You guys have enriched my life with unforgettable characters, and I endeavor to enrich my readers' lives with my stories and unique characters.

And finally, to my loyal readers, you help me to realize my dream, and I will continue to provide you with my very best. I thought of you when I wrote this novel, and I thought of the many avid readers who do not know Christ as their Lord and Savior. I pray that this book will inspire a deeper relationship with God for my fellow believers, and for those who might not know Him, I pray that this book will inspire you to want to have a relationship with God.

Prologue

I realize that I am about to die, and at this moment, I have developed a new power. I'm not talking about powers like X-men; no, I'm talking about a higher sense of the world within me and the world around me. My senses are so keen that I wonder why they haven't kicked in until now.

Take, for example, the view from my room. Every day for the last two weeks I have walked out onto the terrace of my room and gazed at the ocean. I have only been able to see so far, but today, I can almost see the nearest island next to the one I am currently on. I can smell the saltwater from the sea and feel the wind race through my skin. I pour myself a glass of scotch without ice. I know for a fact that it cools as much as it burns while going down. Of course, I haven't had a sip, and it's not like I haven't recently had a drink, but still, there is something to be said about going to meet my Savior having at least challenged my darkest demon. I stare at the glass for what feels like an eternity before I set the glass back down on my desk. Even though I am about to die, and I'm certain that I won't lose my salvation over a drink, I still can't take a drink; not now, not anymore.

I spend a good portion of my life delving in secrets and entertaining the demon elixir. As a result, there aren't too many things that I am proud of in my life. No amount of alcohol could drown out my problems, I see that now, but I also see my end. What's one last drink? I know I said that I wouldn't, but I can't resist.

I pick up the glass and bring the scotch to my nose. It's a decent scotch, but I've had better. It will have to do though. I take the drink, and it satisfies my thirst. Lord, forgive me for being weak and flawed in my hour of temptation.

Since I have already given into one temptation, I take in my other vice. I pick up the pack of smokes I have on my table, and place one cigarette on the edge of my lips.

I savor the taste of the tobacco for a minute before I strike a match that I picked up from the Atlantis Casino. I couldn't resist making a stop along the way to Crystal Cove.

I protect the flame with my hands from the island breeze as I draw it in close and light the end of my cigarette. Then I take in the smoke before I release it into the wind. The day is clear, and the ocean is inviting. It's a good place God picked for me to die.

At least I will die a millionaire, though I didn't get the chance to spend the money. And what's the point? No one knows about the money except my employer. I wish I could give it to charity or to Victory, another thing on my list of regrets.

Any moment now, my killer will arrive. It won't be long now . . . last call. I think about Victory and the last time I saw her. Her eyes were full of disappointment, and it was well deserved. I was rotten to her, and I took something that was special and ruined it. I did it to myself. There is so much I want to tell her, and I can't now. I guess my final lesson before I check out is that I should say the things that I need to say when I have the time to say it. Oh well, what good does regret do for me now? It can't make me bulletproof.

The door clicks open. The hardwood floors snitches on my assailant. It's almost that time. Now my heart is more scared than my mind.

I have to take a deep breath and remain calm. This person may take my life, but they won't take my pride. I won't give them the satisfaction.

The door to my office creaks open.

"I know who you are," I say with my back turned. "I know everything, and I know why you killed him."

I turn around to face my murderer. It turns out to be the person who I suspected. I am right. Boy, how I hate being right, especially now when I am about to die. I hope the information I left will be enough to see this person brought to justice. Now a smirk stretches across my assailant's face, and a 9 mm gun points at my temple. Here we go.

Chapter One

It is eleven forty-six, and he's still not here. Maybe he is a prophet and foresaw that I will be here. I know I couldn't have missed him. There is one main road that goes throughout the island and Doctor Dixon's house is the house that is near the top of the hill. There is someone who lives on top of the hill, but I don't care. I'm waiting for only one person to arrive. Adele, the person whose home I'm staying in, informs me about the affair.

At eleven forty-six, a black Mercedes with black-tinted windows pulls up across the street from Doctor Dixon's driveway. I thought that I wasn't going to get fireworks on this glorious day. Prophet Chambers exits his Mercedes and starts to cross the street. He is alarmed when he sees me, probably for the reason that he has never seen me before today. Prophet Chambers is a six foot four, silver-haired, good-looking gentleman. I can see why so many women find him appealing.

"Can I help you?" Prophet Chambers asks.

"Actually, that's why I'm here, to help you save your ministry," I say.

"And who are you?"

"I'm what the young people call a 'hater,'" I say.

"Listen, young man, I don't have any time for shenanigans. I'm very busy."

Prophet Chambers tries to walk past me, and I stand in his way. He starts to breathe heavily, and he balls his fists.

"Did you know that Doctor Morris Dixon is one of the foremost pediatric surgeons?" I ask.

"Yes, I know. Mr. and Mrs. Dixon are prominent members of my ministry."

"He travels from island to island helping understaffed and underfunded hospitals out. I mean, he's certainly not adequately paid for the services he renders. That's why I think the last thing he would want to hear is the prophet of the church that he attends and writes large checks to is laying healing hands on Mrs. Dixon after-hours."

Prophet Chambers still doesn't know who I am. But he now knows why I am here. His face conveys that he is concerned about me being outside Mr. Dixon's home.

"Who are you?" Chambers asks.

"Someone you'll hate today and thank tomorrow." I put my hands in my pockets and walk up to Prophet Chambers. "I've read up on you. You're actually the real deal. I've read testimonies of little girls with leukemia that were healed. People with longtime illness who are healed once they come to one of your meetings."

"It's a gift God has blessed me with, and I wish I could do something else, but what do you do when you've been called?"

I wish I could answer that question. I myself struggle with my calling. At times, I wonder if I was ever called to ministry. I started helping ministers who wanted to keep scandals from destroying their churches, and years later, I find myself so far away from my original intention.

"God has given you an amazing gift. Don't squander it for the profit of the flesh," I said.

I can tell my words are penetrating Chambers's soul. He looks down at his feet as if he's searching for answers.

"I never meant to go down this road with Phaedra," he says.

"I know," I say. I didn't do a lot of research on Mrs. Dixon, so I assume that Phaedra is her first name.

"But she proves to be a hard woman to resist." Chambers starts to rub his head.

"You need to do what God has placed you on this earth to do . . . and that's help people through the ministry of healing."

"What is going on here?"

I look over Chambers's shoulders and I see Mrs. Dixon walking out to the drive in a silk robe. It doesn't take a genius to see that she probably has on lingerie underneath, if anything at all. Chambers was headed for a fun afternoon before I intervened. Sin costs, and too many of us don't even bother to look at the price tag.

"Who are you?" Mrs. Dixon asks me.

"I'm on vacation, and your husband is on his way home. His last appointment cancelled out early."

That part is not a lie. I found out that the good doctor is headed home and that would make this situation downright murderous.

I've seen too many cases where a man who wouldn't kill a fly one minute, turns around and kills the person that he loves the next minute. A crime of passion is very possible.

I turn to Chambers. "You can do whatever you want. I just hope that you would encourage her to tell her husband the truth and bring an end to this affair in a mature way."

"Do you know him?" Mrs. Dixon asks Chambers while pointing at me.

"He doesn't," I say.

"Will someone talk to me?" Mrs. Dixon says.

"I'm trying to save your marriage and Mr. Chambers's ministry."

"My marriage is none of your concern."

She's right. Mrs. Dixon's marriage is none of my concern. One day I will learn to mind my own business, but today is not that day.

"You can do what you want. I just pray that you would do the right thing," I say to both of them before I turn away.

I start to walk down the hill, and when I look back, I see Chambers trying to talk with Mrs. Dixon and reason with her. Maybe there is hope, but I don't do free jobs, so for me, it's back to my vacation.

I never knew how much I was in need of a vacation until I finally took one. Sitting in a beach chair watching people fish and parasail, the sky has banished the clouds and the wind races past my shoulders.

I know I look like a dork in my cream pants with my white-collar shirt and straw hat, but I don't care. I just continue to eat shrimp the size of a fist and drink a virgin mango daiquiri while reading the latest Michael Connelly book. I like reading mystery novels, even though I can figure out who the murderer is early on in the novel.

I could sit out here all day, but in the back of my mind I know that it won't last; it never does. That's why moments like these are so special. I need moments like this to remind me that it doesn't always rain, and that one does not have to spend life walking through muck and mire. I need this moment since God only knows what lies in the next moment.

Lord knows that when I took the Sacramento job, I didn't expect that I would be tracking down a serial killer, among other things. It was strange enough that the reason I was in Sacramento to begin with was that I was looking for a first gentleman who went missing, only to find out that his wife, the senior pastor, was a former porn star. But that's neither here nor there. I consider myself lucky to come out of that whole ordeal.

I finish my lunch and drift off to sleep, listening to the waves crash the shore and the sound of tourists at play. I dream I am at church. I know it's a dream because I'm wearing jeans, and I don't think I even own a pair of jeans. The church is almost empty, but the presence of God is in full effect. I'm clapping to the music, which is another indication that I'm having a dream since I don't clap or dance in church. I lack the aptitude to do either. The pulpit is empty, and I don't see a preacher. Maybe the open pulpit is meant for me. I'm an ordained minister, but I don't feel like one.

The sound of a horn wakes me from my sleep. I gather myself and recognize the culprit.

A fourteen foot boat name *The Exodus* pulls into the docks. I leave my book behind and start to walk toward the dock. It's a short walk from the palm tree, where I was posted near the dock. The sun makes it difficult to walk barefooted on the sand. I walk along the shore so that the water can cool my feet. I arrive at the dock and up pops Sam Moses. Sam moved to the island after he retired from the water and power company. He now spends his days fishing and selling his catch to the local restaurants.

"Hey, Doc, I see you were napping," Sam says.

"That didn't stop you from waking me up."

"You didn't come here to sleep. You came here to take in the island and all of its fine pleasure. Here!" Sam hands me a cage filled with his catch, and I'm reluctant to take it. "Don't be shy now, take them."

"They seem less hostile at Red Lobster," I say.

Inside the cage are four large lobsters that were plucked from the ocean. Sam sells these lobsters to the restaurants throughout the islands. He doesn't turn a big profit. I hear it said that the Bahamas are the land of lost wealth. Many people come out to the island looking for wealth, something that they never find. I think going out to sea gives him a sense of purpose. A man cannot survive without a sense of purpose.

"You should get a good price for these," I say.

"Oh, these are not for sale. These bad boys are for us. Me, you, and the lovely Adele," Sam says as he steps off the boat.

Adele is not only the woman who I am renting the house from while I am on the island, but she is also the object of Sam's affection.

"I see you're trying to get me caught up in this little coup you've staged for Adele," I say.

"I just don't want her to think that I'm trying to hit on her. I want her to think that it's just a nice dinner between friends."

From what I've been told, Sammy has been hitting on Adele since he came to the islands fifteen years ago. I've only known him for a few weeks, but we walk along shore like we've been friends for years.

"Did I ever tell you about the time I was in California?" Sam asks.

I shake my head, but in truth, Sam has told me this story every day since the time I met him, but Sam tells the story with so much enthusiasm that I just let him go on.

"The Dolphins were in the Super Bowl. Man, my boys just administered a beat down on Washington."

"The final score was only fourteen to seven," I say.

"Hush up, now, it's my story. I let you tell your stories any way you want. Any who, I spent the rest of my time out in Hollywood driving around. You Californians are some strange folks. I saw things there that would make Sodom and Gomorrah blush."

I chuckle at Sam's story, and then take a right onto a trail that leads to a row of homes that sit on the beach.

"So when are you going back?" Sammy asks.

"I don't know, some day, one day before I get used to this." I extend my hand out to an empty blue sky.

"Some things you can never get used to," Sam says. "I've been here fifteen years, and I am still awestruck on days like today."

We just so happen to come across Adele who is taking a stroll with her straw hat and a bag of groceries.

"Good afternoon, Adele," I say.

"Good afternoon, sugar," Adele replies.

"You're looking good, Adele," Sam says.

Adele has on her signature white cotton dress which brings out her mocha complexion.

"Hi, Sam," Adele replies with a crooked smile.

"Adele, Sam caught some lobsters, and I was wondering if we could invite him to dinner tonight?"

Adele mumbles something under her breath. "Okay, Sam, you can come, but we have to be done in time for me to watch my programs. *Justified* comes on later tonight."

I love Adele's thick Bahemian accent. She adds freshness to the English language. She has lived to see her hair evolve from black to gray to silver, a remarkable woman. I lost my grandmother at an early age, too early for me to even appreciate her wisdom.

Adele hands out wisdom like candy, and I am a grateful recipient. She is another reason why I may never go back to the States.

"Nic, I was watching the news this morning," she says to me. "There's a lot of talk about the International Ecclesiastical conference going on at Green Cove. I'm surprised you're not attending the conference, being a minister and all."

The last place I want to be is at a conference. There are over seven hundred islands that comprise all of the Bahamas. The conference is being held on Green Cove, the island next door to the island I'm currently on, Crystal Cove. I chose this island because it's less commercial than the other islands. I did not choose Green Cove for the fact that I didn't want to be anywhere near Pastor Cole. Cole is the leader of the conference and his "God wants us all to be rich" mentality sours my stomach.

"I'm not a big fan of conferences," I say.

My statement doesn't sit well with Adele. I know my directness can come off as harsh, but there is no sense in getting close to someone if you can't be yourself. My deepest desire is to live freely and open, letting everyone see me for who I am.

"Well, let me get to the market so I can get some stuff that can go along with the lobster."

"I can pick up a bottle of wine for today," I say.

"Oh, bless your heart," Adele says before she resumes her trek to the market.

"Yeah, Doc, those walls that Adele has built is about to come crashing down," Sammy says once she is out of earshot.

In my humble opinion, I believe the children of Israel had an easier time bringing down the walls of Jericho.

Later on that night, Adele, Sam, and I sit around an open bonfire, and we eat lobster and drink a bottle of Pinot underneath the stars.

"See, out here, you can get close to God. In the States, man has built skyscrapers, fast cars, and iPhones just so that he can marvel at his own achievements. But out here, you see a wonder that man can't even claim. He just has to sit in awe and observe."

Whenever Sam has a belly full of good food and wine, he turns into a philosopher. Sammy worked for the water and power company, but he spent every waking moment reading and educating his four children into adulthood.

"True, but there is a flip side to the coin," I say. "Skyscrapers and iPhones speak to man's creativity, and thus, divine potential."

"Boring," Adele says after she sips on her wine. "All you men ever want to talk about is God and sports."

"What would you rather us talk about, Adele? *Atlanta Housewives* or *Basketball Wives?*" I ask.

"You," Adele says.

"Me?" I swallow a lump of wine down the wrong pipe and begin to cough. It takes me a minute to recover. "What about me?"

"Every day I see you watch as those planes land, hoping and looking for something or someone. Who is it?"

I don't like talking about myself, and my line of work makes it easy for me to not talk about myself, since I'm always focused on everyone else. I don't have to deal with the demons that lie within me. I pacify them with a paradoxical cocktail of prayer, alcohol, and nicotine.

At least . . . that was the case until now. I gaze into the flames and think of only one person who can make this night perfect.

"Victory."

"Who?" Sam asks.

"She is a woman I met recently, and I gave her an open ticket to fly out here. Each day I wonder if she is on one of those incoming flights."

"She must be a cold piece of work to be named Victory," Sam says, "and you must be the biggest fool I've ever seen to be out here without her."

"I'm trying to tell you," Adele says.

The one time these two agree with each other . . . and it's at my expense. Sam is right.

I am a fool; a fool to think that Victory and I have something special, that my time in Sacramento was not a waste. Love is a cold game, and I'm not ashamed to admit that I don't have the stomach for combat involving matters of the heart.

"She'll come," Adele says, as certain as she is sitting along the fire breathing.

We spend a long time in silence watching the crackling of the fire. It feels good to be in the company of people who can appreciate silence as much as I do.

"What time is it?" Adele asks.

Sammy and I both look down at our watches.

"It's about ten o'clock," I say.

"Oh my goodness, *Justified* is on. Sitting around fooling with y'all two, I almost missed my Raylan Givens."

Adele takes off heading toward her house like an Olympic sprinter.

An hour later the show concludes. Sam was not invited to watch *Justified* so he went on home with the promise that he and I would hook up later.

"Whoo wee, I just love my Raylan Givens, especially when he asks folks if they are willing to bet their life on it."

"Yea, it's a good show." It has a little too much violence for my taste, but I see why Adele finds the show appealing.

"Do you mind if we watch the nightly news?" I ask.

"Sure, sugar." Adele hands me the remote, and I change to the news station.

A breaking news bulletin appears on the scene with a local reporter. I still haven't adjusted to the contrast between the news out in the States and the news on the island. In the U.S., our news primarily focuses on what's going on domestically, while out here in the islands, the news is focused on what's going on internationally.

"Breaking news: tragedy struck this Faith Conference when the keynote speaker Pastor Jeremiah Cole was found dead."

"Oh my Lord," Adele says.

My Lord is right. A famous pastor is found dead on an island next to mine. What could that mean for my vacation?

Chapter Two

I wade in the warm water and let the tame waves pass around my body. With my arms outstretched and my eyes closed, I pray to God for peace, for direction, and on this day, I pray for a fallen comrade, Pastor Jeremiah Cole. In truth, I never liked Pastor Cole. I never got a phone call from his peoples, and he taught a capitalistic view of the scriptures that I vehemently disagreed with. In this day and age, I feel like the people of God need to be made whole more than they need a new Mercedes. Pastor Cole thought different; at least, that is what his sermons suggest. However, I wouldn't wish hell nor suffering on my worst enemy. I pray that Pastor Cole was square with the Lord by the time he checked out of this life and into eternity.

I open my eyes and take one look into the sky and see a clear path to God; nothing in the way except for smoke clouds. I start my day the same way I have started it since I arrived here for vacation. I go for a swim and relax. I cut through the walk, tilting my head from side to side. I feel a slight burn in my legs and arms as I continue to push for another mile until the inside of my body feels like it's consumed by a fire. I then dip underneath the water and observe the multicolor corral reefs before maneuvering my body in the opposite direction.

I come up for air and after a moment of wiping the water from my face, I see that the shore is a short distance away. It won't take long for me to get back, but it's a little more challenging to get back when your energy is spent. I start off well toward the shore, but the burning inside of me comes on quick, and I start to slow down. Here is where my will has to push me past the pain, so I keep pushing, digging, and twisting my head from side to side. My will to reach the shore subdues any pain that I may be feeling at the present moment.

Eventually I arrive at shore with my body exhausted, and that concludes my morning exercise. I lie out on the sand and catch my breath.

"Nic!"

I look up and see Adele waving for me to come in. If there is one thing I love more than swimming, it's Adele's cooking. I regain my breath and do a light sprint up the beach toward the house. Adele has a white two-story house that looks like it was plucked out of the suburbs of North Carolina and landed on the beach.

She has a breakfast nook on her deck that faces the massive Caribbean Sea. Every morning I sit out on the deck with Adele, and we eat our breakfast while enjoying the picturesque view. One would think we were a part of a painting, which sits in one of those upscale Beverly Hills doctors' offices. I walk into Adele's nook and pull out a chair for her.

"Thank you, sugar," Adele says.

"With pleasure," I say after I sit on the opposite side of her and begin to serve us up some breakfast. Adele has made her famous Salmon Croquet along with grits and eggs. She also made freshly squeezed orange juice. After we pray, we break bread. The meal is great, even though today the Salmon Croquet is a little too salty. Adele must've been distracted, and I know why.

"I still can't get my mind off of Pastor Jeremiah Cole," she says.

"Yeah, that's tragic."

"Why would anyone want to kill a man of God?"

"Adele, you'd be surprised. The possibilities are end-less." I am not sure if Pastor Cole is a true man of God or if he was just posing as one. Nevertheless, murder is murder, and the grim details of Pastor Cole taking two shots in the back of the head gives me the chills.

"It's a scary time when folks start killing ministers." Adele got the shakes from her statement.

"It sure is," I say.

"We have to pray for his family. That's a shock, and the deaths you don't expect to happen are a lot tougher to get over," Adele says.

Now I know that I am not Mr. Happy-Go-Lucky. I'm not built that way. I am pragmatic in my approach, and while I believe that all things work together for a greater good, I also believe that life does not fit into a nice bow. With that being said, I have to agree with Adele when she says that we are living in a dangerous time when a preacher can be murdered with little regard of divine consequences.

I hate when I get this feeling, this feeling of duty. All I want to do is enjoy my vacation, but part of me feels like I cannot have peace as long as there are questions looming over me about Pastor Cole. Why would anyone want to kill him? Is the murderer still around?

"You know, I was thinking of going down to the island and paying my respects to Pastor Cole."

"That sounds like a good idea," Adele says.

"What sounds like a good idea?" Sam asks as he ap-proaches the nook from the shore.

"Go away, Sam. Folks weren't talking to you," Adele says.

"We're talking about Pastor Cole," I say.

"Oh yeah, that's some cold business right there." Sam takes off his baseball cap and scratches the back of his head.

"I was thinking about going over to the island next door and paying my respects to Pastor Cole."

"Say the word and we can take my boat," Sam replies.

"Sammy, don't nobody want to get on your cursed boat," Adele says.

As much as I love Sam, Pastor Cole's body would've been sent back to Atlanta, Georgia, where he's from by the time Sam's boat reaches the dock.

"Actually, Sam, time is of the essence, and I'm going to need a flight. Do you know of any charter pilots?"

Adele lets out a laugh as if I have just missed a private joke.

"Yeah, I know someone," Sam says, absent his flair and panache.

"Is he any good?" I ask.

"Whew, Lord!" Adele says.

Adele can't stop laughing and I wondering what is so funny.

"What?" I ask.

"Oh, nothing."

Whoever this pilot is, I hope he can get me to this island in one piece.

Sammy gives me a ride in his pickup truck. The road out in the island is so narrow that an American driver would have a difficult time. Even though the lanes are painted for two cars to travel on, it's easier said than done. There is only one major road throughout the island, and Sam and I took it all the way to Paradise airport.

At the airport, even the landing strip is very narrow, but I watch the plane land perfectly on the runway. I hope that is my pilot because I am very familiar with the stories of Kennedy, John Denver, and Aaliyah.

"Is that my pilot?" I ask.

"Uh-huh," Sam says. His voice still lacks the flair that I have been accustomed to hearing.

The plane's propellers come to a stop, and I get out of the truck and shut the door. I thought that Sam would get out of the vehicle to introduce me to the pilot, but instead, he stays in the truck. I walk toward the plane and see a dark male figure walking toward me. I can only assume it's my pilot.

"How do you know this pilot?" I ask, but before I could turn around to look at Sam for a response, he not only turned on the ignition, but he backed up and pulled away.

"What the heck is wrong with him?'" I ask myself before I turn around and see the dark figure in a pilot uniform within a few feet of me.

"Nic Dungy." He extends his hand, and I shake it. "Hi, I'm Donny Moses."

"That means you must be Sam Moses' . . ." I just made the connection.

"Son," Donny says with more annoyance than gratitude.

There is a story as to why the father and son can't be in the same air space, but that is for another time. Right now, I have to get to Green Cove.

"Are you ready to go?" Donny asks.

"Yes, I am," I say, but I am not sure what I will find when I get there.

Chapter Three

The island looks like a crooked letter *I* from up in the air. The water is more of a teal color with white tips. Back at home, I wouldn't be able to see water that looks like the water that surrounds the Bahamas. Donny maneuvers the plane and aims for a thin landing strip. He touches down on the narrow landing strip with ease. For Donny, I believe it's another day at the office.

"How long have you been flying?" I ask.

"Six years. It always was a dream, but I never decided to pursue it until I got laid off from Boeing after twenty-three years."

Losing a job can be very stressful, but then I hear stories like Donny's and realize that God always has a plan for our lives, even when it seems like the world doesn't. If I had to guess based on what transpired at Crystal Cove airport, Sammy is a touchy subject for Donny, so I won't pry; instead, I'll sit back and enjoy the flight.

"So you're from California?" Donny asks.

I nod my head in agreement.

"Boy, I sure do enjoy watching my Heat beat up on your Lakers."

"Aw, man, just fly the plane," I say.

Donny and I enjoy a few good laughs, and we even get a chance to talk about the Bible before he makes a soft landing onto the landing strip of the Green Cove airport.

"Well, here we are," Donny says as he unfastens his seat belt.

"Thanks so much."

"How long you plan to be here?" he asks.

"I'm only going to be a couple of hours, three at the most."

"Well, I'll be here waiting for you," Donny says.

I hear the sound of a horn, and I look over and see off in the distance a kid with long dreads waving me down as if he knew me. The boy has a motorcycle with a cart attached to it.

"Who is that?" I ask.

"Cameron, a knucklehead-turned-entrepreneur. He calls himself running a taxi service," Donny says while he ties the plane down.

"You know anyone who has ridden with him?"

"No," Donny says without hesitation. "Feel free to risk your life after we clear customs."

I clear customs without any problems, and when I got on the other side of the airport, there is Cameron still waiting for me to hitch a ride on his truck. Even though Donny's answer is disconcerting, I love an underdog, so I decide to approach the young entrepreneur. The closer I get, the wider Cameron's smile grows.

"Good afternoon, fam. Cameron here is the fastest taxi on the entire island."

"I'll be the judge of that. I need to get to the Marquee Hotel pronto," I reply.

"No problem, boss. Cameron will get you there pronto," Cameron says.

"Are you going to refer to yourself in third person the whole ride?"

"Yes, sir," Cameron says.

I shake my head and chuckle to myself as I climb into the two-seat cart connected to Cameron's motorcycle. I didn't even get into the cart all the way when Cameron presses on his accelerator and takes off. I fall back into my seat, and I can hear Donny laughing his butt off in the distance. With nothing more than my pride damaged, I adjust in my seat. I resolve that I will need a back brace before this ride is over because these seats are far from comfortable.

"Hang on, fam. Cameron has everything under control."

I suspect Cameron didn't have anything under control. This island's roads are more developed on this island than on the island that I was on. This road has three lanes, and Cameron uses all three lanes. The motorcycle weaves in and out of the lanes, and the cart follows close behind.

I thank God that Cameron has good enough sense to have the hitch so tight together that I didn't swerve when the cart switches lanes. I will say this, Cameron does not mess around. He is fast and knows the island and the routes well. I can also tell that this island has more corral reef viewpoints and oceans, hence, the name Green Cove, and that makes it more appealing than its less-than-fifty-miles neighbor.

Cameron makes a hard right turn off the main road and down a steep hill. I'm certain this will cause the cart to turn over and I will be sent flying into my death. Cameron, however, remains vigilant and kept both the bike and the cart on course.

We arrive at the bottom of the hill where a hotel sits less than a hundred feet away from the shore. The architecture of the house resembles a state building, and thus, the hotel looks as if it has no earthly business being on the beach. The place isn't crawling with local law enforcement; just a few Jeeps with sirens attached to the roof of the vehicle. This is a place where a gruesome murder of an internationally renowned pastor took place.

Even though there is a police presence at the scene, I notice that the presence is light, and I am somewhat disappointed. I vehemently opposed Pastor Cole on a theological level, but from a humane perspective, a man of his stature deserves more of an outcry. But that is just the way this world is. A lawmaker can spend his entire tenure breaking every moral code and use his power to put his foot on the necks of his constituents, and yet, he receives a military salute and ongoing investigation. I realize that will probably not be the case for Pastor Cole, however. The church community will have a great celebration of his legacy, and preachers from all around will come and try to outdo each other in the best eulogy. There will, without a doubt, be a concert from Gospel-recording artists to choirs, and then silence. The center stage will be empty until the battle over supremacy for Pastor Cole's church is over. That's what awaits Pastor Cole's followers.

"Here you go, fam. Cameron told you I would get you there fast." Cameron bothers himself to open the cart door to let me out.

"Thank you," I say as I stumble to get out of the cart. Though I'm not Catholic, I cross myself as if I was and reach into my pocket and hand him a hundred-dollar bill.

Cameron's eyes light up when he sees the money. "Thank you, fam. If you ever need a ride, you just let Cameron know."

Hopefully, I won't. "Okay, just be careful, all right?"

"Sure!" Just like that, Cameron hops on his motorcycle and guns his bike.

I walk toward the hotel somewhat perplexed. Though this is a luxurious hotel, I have seen Pastor Cole fill up stadiums. I wonder why of all of the places Pastor Cole can have his international conference, he chooses to have his conference here.

I walk past the police officers who aren't doing anything but passing the time. I enter the hotel and see a bunch of people in their uniforms running around. In the midst of a murder investigation, the hotel staff still tries to attend to the whims of their guests. The report says that Pastor Cole was shot and killed in his hotel room. The police officers that are on the inside of the hotel make their way up and down the staircase. Pastor Cole's hotel room must've been in the back because some of the police officers would disappear once they reach the second floor. For a second, one wouldn't think that a murder has taken place, just that the hotel is extremely busy.

The conference is taking place in the back of the hotel, so I make my way past the staircase and the front desk and down a narrow hallway. While planning for this trip, I thought about staying in Green Cove and staying in this very hotel. I am thankful for my decision to go to a more secluded island.

I arrive at the outside of the conference room. Two gentlemen stand guard in front of the closed doors.

"I'm Minister Nicodemus Dungy. I'm here to offer my—"

I couldn't even finish my sentence before the man's eyes enlarged as if I am some kind of a celebrity.

"Right this way, Minister Dungy." The man takes me by the arm before I even have a chance to protest. We cross the lobby and head toward the back of the room.

I enter the conference room and the who's who of ministers are in attendance. I see Pastor Christie from Higher Ground in Philadelphia, a former client. Then there is Pastor Richardson from Milwaukee, seventeen thousand members strong.

I even see Pastor Gerald Watkins from Powerhouse Faith in Chicago, also a former client. The list goes on and on, and my curiosity grows. With this many prominent pastors on this small exotic island, I wonder if there is more going on than just an international convention. I could be wrong, but my track record suggests otherwise.

Pastor William Bryant enters the conference room. He and Pastor Cole are as thick as thieves. No surprise as to why he is here. He has one of the two largest ministries in the country, and he is one of the main keynote speakers. Pastor Bryant is head and shoulders taller than any other man in the room, and he reinforces his stature with a tailor-made power suit. I'm sure he's the envy of his fellow brethren with a full head of hair and only a few gray streaks.

"Good afternoon, gentlemen, men of God. Today is a black day for us all. One of our generals of the Gospel has been sent home to be with the Lord, and it's not his death that troubles me; it's how he died. The devil is strong, but we as men of God are stronger."

"Amen," we say in unison.

Pastor Bryant has a voice that commands attention, and his vocabulary and diction are so precise that I hang onto every word.

If I was still preaching, I would want to be able to command a crowd like Bryant. I know it's shallow and self-conscious for me to say that, but I'm only human.

"The devil is trying to take us out, and the police do not have any suspects, but I know that God will help us to bring to justice the people responsible for this. For the family of Pastor Cole, let us pray."

I bow my head and think about Adele's words regarding Pastor Cole. I'm not a prophet of doom, but to wake up and hear about a pastor being murdered is a sign of the end times in my opinion.

"Amen," we all say upon completion of the prayer.

I look up to see the same short man that led me into the conference room is now whispering in Pastor Bryant's ear. One can only guess what the short man is telling Pastor Bryant because immediately, Pastor Bryant's eyes start scanning the room, and when his eyes lock onto mine, I know what the short man has been whispering to him. A smile creeps out the side of Pastor Bryant's face.

"Oh, Minister Dungy . . . A word in private, please," Bryant says.

All the men turn around to look at me, and I have a look like I have just been called into the principal's office. I emerge from the group and follow Pastor Bryant out of the conference room down the hallway. Bryant doesn't break stride nor does he turn around to check and see if I am following him. He just keeps on walking until he arrives at a door at the end of the hallway. Bryant opens the door like he owns the place, and I close the door behind me. He goes into the minirefrigerator and pulls out a bottle of water.

"Do you believe in serendipity, Minister Dungy?"

"I believe in the scriptures when it says all things work together for the greater good."

"The greater good," Pastor Bryant says to himself. "What are the odds that you would happen to be on this island at the same time Pastor Cole is killed?"

"Am I a suspect in this case?" I ask, not sure of the intentions behind Bryant's line of questioning.

"Quite the opposite. I was thinking more of an asset. Maybe even a saint."

I've been called many things; most of it I won't even bother to repeat, but a saint would undoubtedly be the first.

"Let's cut to the chase. You know who I am and what I do, so what's up?"

"What is your opinion of Pastor Cole?"

"Not a high one," I say.

"Well, contrary to what you see on the news or hear whispered among certain circles, Pastor Cole was an honorable man."

Pastor Bryant's statement is met with silence. I have no way of determining if Pastor Cole was honorable or not. It doesn't really matter to me anyway since he's dead. It's a harsh reality, but I'm not the kind of person who dislikes someone one minute, and then praise them when they die.

"I need your help in finding out who did this," Pastor Bryant says.

It takes a minute for me to realize what Pastor Bryant is asking of me. He wants me to find out who killed Pastor Cole.

"You know they got these guys who run around here with a badge and a gun called cops. They're more qualified to help you in this endeavor—"

"—You know the police are not going to kick over any stones to find a slain pastor's killer. Pastor Cole is one of our own, and you may have forgotten that, but I need a soldier, a man of God with a unique skill set such as yours to bring the person responsible for this to justice."

It hasn't even been a month since my ordeal with the husband stalker. The infamous serial killer avoided authorities for decades. He sought after the husbands of prominent women and brutally murdered them. With the help of my friend and bounty hunter, Spider, we were able to capture him. After my run-in with the husband stalker, I have had my share of chasing after another killer. That was not in my job description.

"I'm not sure what it is you need me to do," I say.

Pastor Bryant goes into his pocket and pulls out a small pen and a tablet and starts to scribble on the paper. Judging by the way he's writing, I assume that he is writing down a figure.

"I just need you to knock on a few more doors and ask a few more questions. And if you do find out who is responsible for this, this will be your reward."

Pastor Bryant folds the piece of paper and hands it to me. I open the piece of paper and at first I think that Pastor Bryant is being a little too cavalier with the zeros, but then I realize that he has over 30,000 members whose tithes and offerings allow him to be carefree with their money.

"This is a lot of money," I say.

"Indeed, but you know I'm good for it," Pastor Bryant says.

"That's not what I'm implying. Pastor Cole must've been in deep for someone to kill him, and by me taking on this assignment, that means I'm about to get in deep as well, so before you pay me a king's ransom, tell me something that those other guys in the room don't know."

Pastor Bryant finishes his water and places his hands in his pocket. "You realize that what I'm about to tell you is of the highest confidentiality."

"If you know me, then you know what I do and you know the answer."

Pastor Bryant nods his head in concession. Even my enemies would vouch for my discretion.

"Have you heard of Randall Knox?"

"The business tycoon who just had an unsuccessful gubernatorial campaign?" That's my way of saying that I know who Randall is, and I know of his influence back home. I also know that he's a jerk and a proud member of the 1 percent. "What about him?"

"After 9/11, Knox noticed a spike in church attendance, but what he also noticed was after the waves of emotions subsided from 9/11, people stopped attending church as usual. So he and his think tank got together and came up with an idea. They started approaching pastors, offering to help them expand their ministries and keep the church pews full. He offers construction companies and franchise coffee shops and fast-food restaurants. The pastors soon saw his genius and saw a way to make a profit."

I remember reading an article not too long ago that showed a cathedral with a golden arch on the outside. It was an article that focused on how corporate America has both infiltrated and influenced today's church.

The article made me sick. I understand why Jesus turned over the money tables. The church is supposed to be a place of prayer and healing, not commerce. I know I'm the last person to judge, but if I walk into the church and see more commerce than prayer going on, then something is off.

"So how does this relate to Pastor Cole?"

Pastor Bryant lets out a big smile. "He was the innovator; he's the first to embrace big business in the church. He changed the game."

"He prostituted the church, you mean," I say without remorse.

"Don't look at it from one angle. There is another side to the coin. Big corporate dollars means more education programs, affordable living programs, work placement programs, and recovery programs. The list goes on and on with what the church can do with enough resources. The church is now able to provide people with not only spiritual nourishment, but socioeconomic nourishment as well. These opportunities no longer lay at the back of the congregational tithes and offerings."

I hear what Pastor Bryant is saying, but the truth is that the church is meant to be sustained by tithes and offerings through the faith of the congregation. The church would always thrive if souls are being saved, even if a Starbucks is not in the lobby.

"So you think one of these corporate execs had Pastor Cole killed?"

Pastor Bryant shrugs his shoulders. "I don't know. All I know is that money is the root of all evil. Lord know what people would do if they stood a chance to gain it or lose it."

"I need a name, something to go off of. The list of suspects stretches from here to Atlanta. Could it be any of the ministers that are here at the conference?"

"No," Pastor Bryant says.

"How do you know? Obviously, whoever did this had access to Pastor Cole."

"Because these are men of God, and they wouldn't do that."

"Oh yeah, because men and women of God don't sin; we all just follow the Bible to the letter. Bottom line, if you live in this world, you get a little dirty."

Pastor Bryant is taken aback by my frankness. I know it's a strong indictment of his fellow brothers and sisters of the cloth, but experience has taught me to never rule someone out.

"The day before he died, Cole came to me visibly shaken. He said he was concerned for his life. He wouldn't tell what or who. All I know was that I saw fear in his eyes."

"And that was the last time that you saw him?" I ask.

Pastor Bryant nods his head. He then pinches his eyes to keep the tears at bay. "I should've pressed the issue, but I didn't. I have to live with that, but I can at least find out the truth of who killed my brother."

The story is compelling, and Pastor Bryant is right: the world won't care what happens to a preacher. But this is my vacation, and I really should be trying to get over what happened in Sacramento. I'm not up for this challenge, but I can't ignore the urge within that is telling me to pursue this case. I don't know if it's the devil or the Holy Spirit. All I know is that it's a voice that I cannot ignore.

"I'll ask around and see what I find."

"There's one more thing. Cole would kill me if I told you this." Bryant goes into his pockets and scribbles something on another piece of paper.

He hands the paper to me, and I read it. It says Elisha Davis and it has her address written at the bottom of the paper. "Pastor Cole had a daughter from back when he was in seminary a long time ago. That was part of the reason why he had the conference out here, to see her. Look her up and see what she might know."

So Pastor Cole had a daughter that the world didn't know about. Every man has his vices, and every man has his secrets.

"And before I forget," Bryant goes into his jacket and hands me an envelope. "Make sure you hand this to her. I would do it myself, but since you're going to see her first . . ."

More than likely there is a check on the inside of this envelope. The question is, is this check for a grieving daughter, or is this hush money?

"Okay, I will probably start there and ask her a few questions."

Pastor Bryant shakes my hand before he heads toward the door.

"What are you going to do?" I ask.

"The conference must go on. The devil can't win."

He's right; the devil can't win, but to continue with a conference in the midst of Pastor Cole's death is bad form.

I thought about Pastor Bryant's words on the flight home. I arrive at Adele's place to hear her engage in a playful conversation. I don't want to be rude and not say anything so I go into the kitchen and there in the middle of the living room is Victory. Victory has finally arrived, and her timing couldn't have been worse.

Chapter Four

Victory's hair looks like it's been kissed by fire. Her hair is also stringy like I remember. She wears a cream sundress that fits her slim frame to a tee, and the scent of cucumber melon permeates from her skin. In short, Victory's presence is both refreshing and breathtaking.

"Boy, if you don't pick your mouth up off my floor, I'm going to kick it closed," Adele says.

Victory covers up her mouth in laughter to avoid adding to the embarrassment that Adele's comments causes. But she doesn't have to cover up for my sake; I love to see her smile, even at my own expense.

"You look good, Nic," Victory says.

I'm glad I don't look the way that I feel. "Thank you. You're beautiful, as always."

"Lord Jesus, gets this boy some game. I swear!" Adele says.

Victory tries to cover up her laughter again, but can't. I understand Adele is quite a character.

"I've been comparing notes with Adele," Victory says.

"Hopefully, she hasn't been beating me up too bad," I reply.

"No, but I did tell her how you've been out here watching the planes as they come in like Tattoo on *Fantasy Island*. It was starting to get embarrassing, if you ask me."

Now that statement is a blow to my ego. Whatever swagger points I earned while in Sacramento has just been lost in a matter of seconds. Adele sits there and dares me to challenge her on her accusations. Of course, I have a weak defense, so I must continue to take the blows.

"Sorry to keep you waiting. I didn't know I was in such high demand," Victory says.

"You have no idea," Adele states.

"Excuse me," I say to Adele, and I extend my hand to Victory. She takes my hand and grabs her purse. Victory leaves her suitcase behind and follows me. Out of my peripheral vision, I can see that Adele wants to protest, but she decides to just let us go. I'm sure Adele will have plenty of time to compare notes with Victory, but since I arrived at this island, I couldn't wait for Victory to show up so that we can walk along the sand. I wonder if she will get the same pleasure from feeling the warm sand between her toes.

"I didn't think you'd come," I say.

"I must've thought about getting on that plane a million times, but I didn't." Victory takes her sandals off and holds them in her free hand.

"Are you going to spare me the suspense?"

"I don't know. I guess since things went well in Sacramento, I thought that it might be better to leave it be. You know how they say some people come into your life for seasons. Maybe that was our season."

"But?"

"I hate what-ifs. I really do. I hate what-ifs about as much as I hate an open-ended ending to a love story. I want a clear conclusion, and I hate leaving a handsome man on an island all by himself."

I too hate what-ifs and believe in seeing things through to the end. I build my reputation off of several principles, and that was one of them. I don't know if the rules that govern my career can also apply to my dating life, but then again, I don't know any other way to do things.

We walk along the shore and don't talk for a while. We just look out at luxury cruise liners and speedboats as they cut through the calm waters.

"Adele says that you went over to the island where Pastor Cole was murdered."

"Yeah, I went by."

"Brutal. A famous pastor like that gets murdered at a church conference, of all places. We are definitely in the end times."

We have been in the end times for a while now, the devil has been running rampant, and if there is anything I can do for the betterment of the kingdom, then here I am, Lord, send me.

"Are you okay?" Victory asks.

No, I am not okay. I would've been okay if I hadn't watched the news the other night. I wish I would've come home from hanging out with Sammy and found Victory in Adele's living room and all I have to worry about is if Victory is having a good time. But, no, I find myself in the midst of this murder case. "Yes, I'm okay; it's just that I got to go by and see this girl as a favor for a friend, but I don't want to leave you alone."

"Well, I can come along. I haven't had a chance to see the island."

"Actually, this is a delicate matter, and only I can handle it directly. You know, pastoral stuff. But I promise I'll be back before you even know I'm gone."

Victory looks perplexed as to why she couldn't tag along, but she didn't say anything. I guess she didn't want to give the sense of being jealous.

"Well, no problem. Adele says that she wants to give me a tour of the island. I would like to get her perspective of this place."

Adele is a lifesaver in this instance. I take Victory by her hands and kiss them. "We'll meet up for dinner, and I promise, no more distractions."

"Nic, one thing about me that you might not know. You don't have to constantly make promises to me. Only promise the things that you can deliver on. Deal?"

Why did I do that? Why did I promise something to Victory? I make a point never to promise something that I can't deliver, and given this present set of circumstances, I can't even promise that I will make it to dinner on time.

"Deal," I say.

"Hurry back, because we have a lot of catching up to do," Victory says.

She leaves me with her dress blowing in the wind as she walks toward Adele's house. I pray that I'm not away from her long.

I arrive at Elisha Davis's house unsure of what to say to her. It shows how small the world is when on an island with a population of less than 2,000, there is the love child of a slain pastor. I have been on this island for two weeks, and I have seen most of the Ten Commandments broken with very little regard to God's authority. I guess this is as good of a place as any for a child out of wedlock to hide.

Her home is small by most modern homes' standards, but a small home in the middle of paradise trumps a two-story home in the heart of the city any day. I'm not sure how I am going to play this situation out. I'm thinking about letting the flow of the conversation dictate the course. The doorbell does not work, so I knock on the door. After some rumblings, the door finally opens.

"Hello," Elisha says in a thick Caribbean accent.

"Hello, Elisha Davis, my name is Minister Nic Dungy, and I'm here on behalf of Pastor Cole's last request."

Elisha remains stoic. I mean, the news did have an impact, but not much. Maybe I'm expecting a little more from a girl who just lost her father. Regardless of how strained the relationship was between the two, Pastor Cole was still her father. Elisha took another moment to size me up. I can tell that she isn't sure if I'm someone that she can trust.

"Come on in," Elisha says and opens the door.

If no one told me that Elisha is Pastor Cole's daughter, I wouldn't have guessed. There is a case that could be made for the full lips and nose that resembles Cole's, but even her complexion is a shade darker than the coffee skin of Cole.

I enter the home, and Elisha makes a beeline to the kitchen. The living room is full of family portraits. Pastor Cole is missing from all of them, of course. It's safe to assume that Elisha must've had her name changed to her mother's last name.

It's a full-time job covering up the past. Who knows what else Pastor Cole kept from the public's eye? I wonder what was Pastor Cole hiding that cost him his life.

These pictures can't answer those questions for me. I suspect that if there are any pictures of Elisha with Cole, those pictures are hidden from plain sight. There are a list of accomplishments that stop with Elisha graduating from Florida A&M. Her accomplishments tell a story that Pastor Cole's influence and money had a hand in telling.

"Here you go," Elisha comes back into the living room with a glass of lemonade.

"Thank you." I'm not much of a lemonade drinker. I prefer ice tea, but it is rare to meet a girl like Elisha who still has manners. We sit down on a couch.

"So you knew my father?"

"No, I didn't. I met him a couple of times, but that was it." I took a sip of the lemonade and set it down on the coffee table in front of me. Not bad, a little too tart, but for someone who used to drink Jack Daniels for breakfast, I can manage.

"You must have a high opinion of him to be here on his behalf."

"Not really," I say without any hesitation.

"Neither did I; at least you're honest. So why are you here?"

I have forgotten that there is an envelope inside my jacket pocket. I reach in and hand it over to Elisha. Elisha doesn't waste any time opening it. She scans the letter and the check that is attached. I expect to see a smile on her face; instead, she looks perplexed. Elisha's perplexity morphs into anger without warning.

"Is this a joke?" Elisha turns the check around and shows me a payment made out to her for $1 million.

I swallow wrong, and the tartness of the lemonade makes me pay for it. I cough several times before I regain my faculties. "Excuse me?"

"This is only *half* of what I was promised. Where is the rest?"

I'm floored at this point, because I made it a rule not to enter a room uninformed, and I must be the smartest person in the room. I allowed Pastor Bryant to let me walk into a room where I am short on both, and now I need to try to grasp the gravity of the situation.

"Let's relax and calm down. I'm sure there's a reasonable explanation for this."

"Unless you have another check on you for $1 million, there is nothing to explain. All I need you to do is go and get me my money." Elisha cocks her head to the side.

The island hospitality has left, and I'm still spinning my wheels. I took another sip of my lemonade before I set it down again and squared up with Elisha.

"It's good to see that you are taking your father's death real hard."

"Do you see any father-of-the-year trophies around here? His money and his time were all that was ever worth anything to me."

"Okay, let's be honest here. What do you expect to accomplish? You expose your father and maybe write a tell-all book, but that's it. Your fifteen minutes are up." I point to the check. "That story is certainly not worth two million. You may be able to get a half of million. but that's it. That's enough money for a clean slate. Take it."

I don't know why I am going to bat for Pastor Bryant, seeing that he is trying to rip off a young girl. At this point, I want to put my hands around his throat for playing me.

"Obviously, you don't know what's going on, so why don't you go back to Reverend Slick Daddy and tell him either he pays me what I'm owed or I'll talk."

What could Elisha have that is more incriminating than the fact that Pastor Cole had a child out of wedlock? My guess, Elisha has something on Pastor Bryant. Why else would Bryant pay so much money to cover up another man's secret?

"Your father was murdered. Aren't you scared for your own safety?"

Elisha just gives me a smirk. "No, not at all. People know not to try anything on me."

"And why not?" I ask.

"Don't worry about all that. I'm not worried; I can take care of myself."

A quick chill shoots through my body. Elisha delivers that line with the upmost confidence. She has someone protecting her, but that someone was not protecting her father. *Why* is a common question that keeps coming up for me, and I don't have any answers.

"What about your mother?" I ask.

The mention of Elisha's mother causes her to pause and reflect. It's clear that she doesn't share the same sentiment toward her mother as she does for her father.

"This isn't about my mother."

"If your mother is around, I'm sure she would advise that this money is more than enough."

"My mother died six years ago, so at this moment, I no longer have a parent to advise me on anything. So from this moment forth, I choose what's enough and *this* . . ." Elisha holds up the check, "*this* is not enough."

For years, Elisha has had to have her wants and desires put on the back burner; not any more. Her father got what he wanted; a hidden secret that remained hidden, but what Elisha wants is to live comfortably.

"Now, you have your orders. Be a good boy and go back to Reverend Slick and tell him he better double the amount or else I talk."

I didn't have a smart retort. I head toward the door with my hat in hand. I just got schooled by a girl who is in her midtwenties at best. I decide to take what's left of my pride and go. A burning question is still on my mind. "You said his money and his time. How often did he ever visit you?"

"He would only visit once a year. He could only stay for an hour, but for that one hour, I didn't feel like a messed-up kid."

I know exactly what she means as I walk out of the door. If it weren't for my messed-up father, I wouldn't have been a messed-up kid who becomes a confused adult that thinks he can save someone other than himself.

Later on that night I went to dinner with Sammy, Adele, and Victory at my favorite restaurant on the island. Auroras is a restaurant by the beach. Most of the tables are outside so the patrons can enjoy their meals under the stars. I wouldn't want to be here during hurricane season, but tonight is a perfect night. There is a gentle breeze, and the night sky is full of stars.

I keep replaying my visit with Elisha in my head. There is something off about the situation. Even though her relationship to her father was estranged, Pastor Cole was still Elisha's father. For her not to be concerned over his apparent murder is unsettling, to say the least. Furthermore, she seems unmoved or unconcerned over her own safety.

"Earth to Minister Dungy." Victory's words snapped me out of my trance and back to the spirited conversation that is happening around me.

"I'm sorry. I was lost in my own thoughts."

"We were talking about Pastor Cole and his ministry and who might've killed him," Victory says.

A pretty morbid conversation to have over fish, but then again, I can imagine a murder occurring on a neighboring island is rare and how that would be the talk of the town.

"What about it?"

"We were just saying that the devil hates success in the Kingdom and with a worldwide ministry, who knows how many greedy people were after him," Adele says.

"Did he really have an international ministry?" I ask.

The group gives me a quizzical look. I know the question seems absurd, but it's not.

"Yes, he had churches in Africa, Afghanistan, and Europe," Sammy says.

"Do you know what a satellite church is? They set up a big flat-screen TV in a room and Pastor Cole preaches to them, and they collect an offering. What I find funny, well, not really funny but interesting, is of all the testimonies of people with fancy cars, big homes, and obese bank accounts, none of them have come from one of these satellite churches. It's a lot easier to preach prosperity in a land that's fueled by greed."

"Who says people in Africa need a Rolls-Royce?" Sammy Moses says. "People use their faith for different things. Some people use their faith to build, while others use their faith to endure."

"But I think the point that is getting lost is the fact that the Gospel is being preached. Who cares if it's being done through a flat-screen television set up in a hut in Nairobi?" Victory asks.

"Maybe that's because there are a lot of homes in Nairobi that don't have a television, let alone a flat screen," I say.

"Doc, you're arguing semantics. The bottom line is that Pastor Cole was about building the Kingdom."

"Oh, Pastor Cole was about building. Building a bigger building," I say.

"And how many buildings have you built through your ministry? Don't criticize a man for doing something, unless you endeavor to do better," Adele says.

That stings to not have an answer to Adele's question. My friends shook their heads at my cynicism. I must've gotten too comfortable because usually I do a better job of concealing my sentiments. At the same time, I can't always be cloak-and-dagger.

"I'm just saying that sometimes people don't need a new car. They just need to know that there is a better life available. Everything else is a distraction from the true meaning of the Gospel," I say.

"And in that regard, I don't think there's that much of a difference between you and Cole," Victory says. "In the end, we're different parts in the same body."

Victory receives a round of applause from everyone at the table. She may have a point, and, in truth, I can go on for hours and debate with her, but my attention has been directed to the man on the other side of the restaurant whose attention is set dead square on us. I know that he can't possibly be listening to our conversation, given that the restaurant is somewhat busy. And there's no way he could pick up on our conversation from where he's standing. From where I'm sitting, I see that the man has dreads that go all the way down his back. His black skin makes his bloodshot eyes stand out.

I am always alert and aware of my surroundings; that is both my gift and my curse. There are some things I don't want to notice, like this gentleman with the dreads in his mustard-colored two-piece suit. I'm uneasy, and I know that I'm not being paranoid. Victory snaps her fingers to get my attention again.

"Are we boring you?" she asks.

"No, I'm just reflecting on what Pastor Cole could've been involved in that would've caused someone to murder him."

"Lord, we came here to eat, not play Angela Lansbury," Adele says.

"Well, I know one thing that will be a mystery we will be debating over for years. Not too many stones will be turned over for a preacher. This generation doesn't believe in anything it can't create," Sammy says.

"Yeah, the world has become a much-scarier place now. I don't know what to tell these young folks other than to believe in Jesus and walk with Him," Adele says.

"I know when I do volunteer work at the local schools, I can't even relate to these kids and what they're going through. I don't know what to say to them but to follow God," Victory says.

"But most people don't know what it means to follow God. To be Christlike, they can't see the rewards. With all due respect, that's why I vehemently oppose pastors like Cole. We can't expect for anyone to grow healthy spiritually if we're too caught up in the materialistic rewards," I say.

"I know this much, there weren't any school shootings in my day. Of course, we used to say a prayer at the beginning of the day too," Sammy says.

I check out the room, and the unnerving individual has not only gotten up from his table, he is making his way toward us.

"Excuse me, but I couldn't help but to notice your conversation, and I was wondering if I could join you?" that man asks.

"You noticed our conversation from where you were sitting?" I ask.

My question causes my new mysterious friend to cut me with his eyes. I don't flinch; instead, I just sit back with a mean look of my own. He chuckles and tries to downplay my question.

"No, you can't," Adele says with certain sharpness. "You're not welcomed here."

It appears Adele knows this gentleman and has the same reservations I have with him. So far, Adele is winning in the meanest-look contest.

"Now go on back to where you came from Demetrius. We don't want the likes of you over here bothering us."

"Adele, don't be rude now," Sammy says before he turns to Demetrius. "Go-ahead and have a seat. I apologize for my friend."

"I don't need nobody apologizing for me, you hear? I don't want to be in the presence of a man like him." Adele points at Demetrius, and now I am curious as to who this individual is and why Adele has such a disdain for him.

"It's quite all right. I understand that my business may cause some concern, but I can assure you that I'm square." Demetrius takes a seat.

"And what is your business, Demetrius?" I ask.

Demetrius turns his evil look toward me. Whatever is the reason why he is here, it's not for anyone to get to know him.

"I am in the export business," he says.

Now that is a bold-faced lie. He didn't do any of the gestures, but his delivery is pitch-perfect. A man on the up-and-up is thrown off when someone accuses him of being otherwise. Demetrius is not the slightest fazed by Adele's accusations. If I have to guess, Demetrius dabbles in the drug trade. I know it's awful to assume that a black man from the island is a drug dealer, but Demetrius doesn't strike me as an honest businessman.

"Whew, the devil is a liar." Adele starts to fan herself.

"Export, that seems very profitable out here," Victory says.

"The truth is I've brought prosperity to Crystal Cove. And my vision is for this place to be as modern as anywhere else in the world."

Adele groans, not wanting to sit through any more of this conversation. "I'd rather see this island go back into the dark ages than to see it built on blood money. Now go on and get."

Now *that* comment enraged Demetrius; at least his eyes showed rage while his posture remains intact. If things were to escalate, I could kick Demetrius in the shin and use my knife I have in front of me, but I couldn't predict the outcome would be in my favor. I'm not even in the same weight class as Demetrius. He's at least two hundred and sixty-five pounds of solid muscle.

"I would dare you to find money that doesn't have blood on it." Demetrius breaks the tension with a smile. "My competitors like to spin stories about me, but the truth is, I have done what is considered the impossible. I have created wealth in the islands."

"Is that what you've done?" I ask.

"Certainly. The islands are known as a place of buried wealth. For someone such as me to come from humble means and become a success intimidates most."

"You soiled your family's legacy. They were good, honest folks, but that wasn't enough for you," Adele says.

"With all due respect, ma'am, you don't know my family's history."

"I knew your family. Your father ran a fishing business by the docks. Now *he* was an honest businessman," Adele says.

"I'm an honest businessman as well."

Adele leans forward and looks at Demetrius with all seriousness. "You can call yourself whatever you want, but I know who you really are and how you got your wealth. Do you want me to call you by your *real* name?"

Demetrius lets out a chuckle for what I assume is to kill the tension and throw absurdity on top of Adele's claim. "I don't want to ruin your evening. That's not my intention, but I just wanted to come by and offer some advice."

"And what's that?" I say, still in attack mode.

"You know what they say about the islands?" Demetrius asks before he pulls out a cigar, lights it, and smokes it.

"What's that?" Victory asks.

I can only assume that Demetrius did this for dramatic reasons. He waits. He does not answer the question right away. Instead, he takes a couple of puffs and allows the smoke to escape from his lips.

"They say it's the land of buried wealth," Demetrius answers.

"And why is that?" I ask.

"Be careful where you dig around here. Truth is, most people come to these islands looking for buried treasure and wind up getting buried."

Demetrius's eyes did not stray from me as he made his statement. I might not be the smartest man in the world, but I'm certainly not the dumbest. And I do recognize a threat on my life when I hear one.

Chapter Five

The next morning I wake up like I have done before for the past two-and-a-half weeks and stand at the shore. Only this time, Victory is standing right beside me, taking in the delightful air and warm water. My thoughts are not on just the prayer, nor are they on how exquisite Victory looks in her one-piece bathing suit and sarong. No, my thoughts keep going back to Demetrius and his subtle . . . and very real threat. I need to go back to the island and deliver Elisha's message as well as ask Pastor Bryant a few questions.

"Come on, slowpoke," Victory says.

Victory gives me a slight nudge from her hips. I open my eyes to see the wind carry her sarong away while Victory immerses herself in the water and starts swimming. I follow after her. It doesn't take me long to realize that Victory is not a casual swimmer, but a swimmer who has spent time in the competitive world of swimming. I'm a fast swimmer, but I have to dig deeper and push harder just to catch up with her. I'm getting more of a workout than usual.

I've been trying to catch up with Victory since the time I've met her. She went through life with her eyes wide open, both to the beauties and the horrors of the world. Victory attacks each day with a ferocious appetite to live and to live out loud. In so many ways I envy her and wish that if only for a moment I could have the same spirit and joy she possesses.

We continue on for about three-fourths of a mile until Victory decides to pause to catch her breath. We tread water in the middle of the ocean. The water is still warm, the ocean has a breeze, and the sky is open.

"You didn't know I have skills?" Victory says.

"I don't know a lot of things."

"Neither do I," she says.

"Why me? Why would you take a sudden interest in me?" I ask.

"Why not you?" Victory shoots back.

"You're going to answer the question with a question?" I ask.

"No, I'm going to let you answer your own question."

Victory dips her head under the water, and then pops back up and wipes the water from her face.

"And why would I answer my own question?"

"Because it's more fun that way."

I don't budge. I like to hold my ground, but oddly enough, I'm in an environment where there is no firm ground. I have to tread water.

"I find the causal question-and-answer thing boring," Victory says.

"So you're all about thinking outside of the box?"

"Correction, in my world, there is no box," Victory smiles.

How does one become so daring and graceful? That is a question that may remain elusive to me.

"I don't know. I saw you, and I said, 'This is a handsome anointed man of God in need of a good laugh.'"

I chuckle right on cue, which further proves Victory's point.

"I laugh, maybe not all the time, but I do laugh."

"No, you chuckle because that's the appropriate thing people do when someone says something funny, but when was the last time you let laughter invade your whole being?"

She's got me there. I can't remember the last time I laughed in God knows how long. Victory splashes water in my face.

"See, that's what I'm talking about. You think too much."

"You may be right, but what about you, Victory? What do *you* want?"

"I want to lay my head back and let the water run through my hair." Victory lays her head back and closes her eyes. We both feel the warmth on our skin.

It doesn't take much to realize what Victory wants out of life. She wants to be present at all times. My envy toward her is as strong as my attraction to her.

"That's all you want?"

"Our biggest problem comes from wanting too much. Then we act like spoiled children when we don't get our way," she says.

"There's nothing wrong with wanting things," I reply.

"No, but we should always be thankful for the moment."

Victory dips her hair back into the water again, and then she locks eyes on me once more. "All I want right now is to beat your butt in another race."

Victory takes off and starts swimming back to shore. She really has to learn how to follow the rules, or maybe I have to learn that Victory is not racing to win, she is racing to live in the now. I put up a better showing, but I still lose the second race.

"That was fun," Victory says as she walks up and retrieves her sarong. I take her by the hand, and we walk up to Adele's house.

Victory is occupying the upstairs room across from mine. Adele's room is downstairs on the opposite side of the kitchen. She has made it clear that there is no shacking up in her house.

"So what are we going to do today?" Victory asks.

"I actually have to go to Green Cove and take care of a few things," I say.

"So what time are we leaving?"

"Actually, this is a solo mission. It will only take a couple hours, and I'll be back before you know it," I say.

"Oh no, you're not about to leave me again. Now yesterday I know I caught you off guard, but today is a different story."

I have no intention of leaving Victory, but I have work to do. "It will only be for a couple of hours."

"Then it will only take a couple of hours. I love Adele and everything, but I didn't come all the way down here to spend time with her. Now you have business to conduct, that's fine, but I'm coming with you. I'll try to be as discrete as possible."

In one swift motion, I take Victory by the hands and kiss them. How can I say no to her? I can't, and that's a dangerous thing. Especially when I'm trying to find out who murdered Pastor Cole.

"Sure, I just have a few boring meetings, but you can tag along."

"Excellent. It sounds like fun," she says.

I chuckle and shake my head as Victory and I walk up to Adele's deck.

"Why don't you go on ahead and get started with breakfast. I have a few phone calls to make."

"Okay," Victory says as she walks over to Adele.

I wave at Adele as I go into the house. I'm glad that I have no reason to try to sneak upstairs because Adele's stairs squeak so loudly that anyone on the island can hear me walking up the stairs. Once upstairs in my room I grab my cell phone. Even on vacation, the rest of the church world continues to struggle with potential scandals. My phone is inundated with missed calls and voice mail messages. The mere sight of the phone causes exhaustion. How many people need help with their problems? I placed my phone on silent when I arrived because I didn't want to be disturbed.

From the window in my room I have a view of the ocean. I can't quite pick up the smell of the sea, but it is awe-inspiring when I look at it. I think about not going back to the States.

I could get citizenship here, which would be an agonizing process, but I don't think Adele will mind me staying on a permanent basis so long as I agree to watch *Justified* religiously and keep Sammy Moses at bay.

Maybe Sammy and I can go into business together, but that's just a thought. The thought of being on the other side of the world away from Victory is what keeps me from staying here. It's not that we are an item; we haven't even had *that* discussion. But that is neither here nor there; right now, I'm in the room for one purpose and one purpose only, and that is to call my friend Paul from the *LA Times*.

"So Nic Dungy finally decides to come up for air and give his friend a call," Paul says.

"Hey, Paul, how are you?"

"Same old, same old. I'm fighting an uphill battle against bloggers."

"Listen, I need a favor," I say.

"What else is new?"

I laugh; I guess Paul and my friendship is predictable. Oh, well, I can't be a great friend to everyone. This is why my list of friends is so short.

"I need you to look up someone for me, a guy by the name of Demetrius Turner. He's an island-born, self-made businessman."

"What kind of trouble you've gotten into now?"

"Nothing I can't handle."

"Okay, I'll give you a cookie and look into this for you."

"I need this information ASAP."

"Um, no," Paul snaps back.

"It's important," I say.

"Look, I already have one annoying boss; I don't need a second one."

I know that I ask a lot of Paul, but this can literally be life or death for me. The information Paul uncovers can crack this whole case wide open.

"This wouldn't have anything to do with Pastor Cole's death, now, would it?" As usual, Paul is always abreast of what is happening both Stateside and abroad.

"Maybe, why? What are you hearing?"

"The popular theory is that his associate had something to do with it. He stands to inherit an empire that Cole built."

I know Pastor Stevens. He lived in California, and we ran in the same circles until Pastor Cole offered him the associate pastor's position. I doubt that this has anything to do with Pastor Stevens wanting to become senior pastor.

"I know I'm wasting my breath, but be careful. It sounds like there is a lot of shady stuff revolving around Pastor Cole's death. The last thing I need is to read about you coming up dead or missing."

"I will."

Of course, that's a lie I tell myself. In truth, trouble always knows where I stay. If Demetrius is anywhere near the dangerous character that I think he is, then I'm going to need to be wise in how I both approach and deal with him. I try to not let the possibility of people close to me being hurt deter me from being able to complete my assignment.

I try to look outside my window and remind myself that I'm in paradise, and that there is no need to worry. I try . . . and I fail. When I head downstairs, I try to take in the laughter and witty banter that is going on back and forth between Sammy Moses and Adele.

"Hey, Doc, how are you?" Sammy greets me.

"Fine," I say before I go over and give Adele a kiss on the forehead.

I take a seat next to Victory, and I give her a kiss on the hands.

"I was just telling Victory that she needs to take a ride on my boat," Sammy says.

"And I was just telling her that if she wants to live to be an old woman, then she must stay clear away from Sammy and his cursed boat."

"My boat is not cursed," Sammy snaps back.

"That's not what the witch doctor says. She says she cursed your boat and anyone who dares steps foot on it."

Sammy is sent reeling by Adele's accusation. I enjoy watching these two go at it like aging prizefighters.

"Now, Adele, you're a Christian woman and shouldn't be talking about no witchcraft," Sammy says.

"What? I'm telling the truth. Don't be mad at me because you're cursed."

"For the last time, woman, I ain't cursed."

"All I know is that strange things happen whenever you are on that boat, like the time when you got struck by lightning without a cloud in the sky."

"Well, that's just a freak occurrence," he says.

"What about the fact that the boat done sunk three times—without a single hole in it?" Adele asks.

"That's a bit of an exaggeration. It only sank twice, and who knows what could've caused it."

"I know *exactly* what done caused it. Your crazy self done messed around with that witch doctor and now until you do right by her, everything you touch will sink." Adele turns to Victory. "You best stay far away from Sammy and his cursed boat."

All Sammy can do is give Adele a dismissive wave. Victory makes no attempt to hide her laughter. She glances over at me. I bet she wonders why I'm not enjoying this elderly couple argue in the middle of paradise. That's because, once again, I find myself thrown into the fray—doing the one job that I seem best suited for, and that is why I can't be present in the moment, enjoying a good laugh.

"Ooh, Sammy, you were going to have me get on a cursed boat?" Victory asks.

"No, Love, I would never put you in harm's way."

"You better off getting that boat Gilligan and them got on," Adele says.

The whole table has a nice laugh at Sammy's expense.

"Anyways, what are you guys planning to get into?" Sammy asks.

"Actually, we need to book a charter flight. I was thinking of giving your son a call."

Sammy pretended like his orange juice went down the wrong pipe. I have to remind myself that before I leave this island, I need to get down to the bottom of the beef between Sammy and his son Donny.

"Well, I'm sure if you give him a call he'd be willing to help you out," Sammy says.

"Actually, I was wondering if you could give us a ride to the airport," I ask.

This time, Sammy *really* was choking on his juice until Adele gave him a good hard slap on the back.

"Well, I would love to help you, Doc, but my transmission is slipping, and I need to get it looked at."

"That's funny, because you offered to take me on a ride around the island yesterday," Adele says.

Adele and I have put Sammy in the corner with nowhere to hide.

"Okay, I'll drop you guys off, but I have to be honest. My brakes are going out, so please forgive me if I don't come to a complete stop before I let you guys out."

The flight went as smooth as it did the first time around. Even though this is not the first flight I made with Donny, it still feels like it's my first flight with Victory on board.

She marveled at the sight of the islands. I wish I had time to take Victory to the different islands so that she can enjoy and marvel at their splendor up close, and I could enjoy and marvel at her.

When we land, Donny escorts Victory off the plane, and then waits for me to walk off.

"That's a special girl you have, Doc," Donny says.

I watch as Victory scans the airport with a smile and a look of curiosity. *Special* doesn't begin to describe her.

"You don't have to tell me. I already know."

"Let's get you cleared through customs and send you guys on your way."

No sooner than we clear customs do I hear a honk, and from the distance I see Cameron waving us down.

"Who's that?" Victory asks.

"A maniac that almost got me killed. We'll catch a cab."

"He acts like he knows you."

"He acts like he knows everybody. That's his whole get down."

Victory takes me by the hands and tries to calm me down. "Listen, I want to spend time with you, but I know that you have some business to take care of first. But if this person can get us there, then let's give him a second chance. Besides, where do you see a cabdriver like this in the States?"

You *don't* see cabdrivers like Cameron in the States, and that's for good reason. I cringe at the thought of

Cameron being in New York or New Jersey or California where the drivers are known for being aggressive. He would cause accidents left and right.

"Hey, fam, good to see you," Cameron says.

I wish I could say the same thing. "Good to see you as well," I lie.

"Where you headed? Cameron will get you there in no time."

Victory looks at me, and I wave off any notion she has of asking why Cameron refers to himself in third person. We hop in the cab and, like before, Cameron guns his bike and takes off. Only difference is, instead of screams, I hear Victory's laughter. I would've thought that we are on a roller coaster.

"Hold on, fam!" Cameron yells as he makes a steep turn down the hill. I feel like we're going to crash, but Cameron maintains just enough control to keep us from crashing . . . just like before. I realize that Cameron didn't take my advice to choose another profession, and it's useless at this point.

Yesterday when I arrived at this hotel, it, at least, had a small police presence. Today, it's a ghost town. Nice to see that the long held theory that not too many people would shed a tear over a dead preacher holds true.

"Beautiful. Is this where Pastor Cole stayed?" Victory asks.

"Yes, this is where he stayed and had his conference every year."

"So sad, but he couldn't have picked a better place to host the conference."

We walk up to the front entrance. The two doormen open the doors for us like we are royalty. I enter in the hotel, and unlike the outside, the inside is pretty busy, which means the conference is in full swing.

"I tell you what, why don't you go have a daiquiri at the bar, and I'll catch up with you in a little bit." I release my grip, but Victory still holds my hand.

"Hurry back, okay?"

For a moment I forget what is so important that I have to leave Victory's side, and then I remember that there is a dead pastor with a hefty payday in it for me. All I have to do is find any info that leads to the murderer of Pastor Cole.

I cross the lobby and move past the receptionist desk toward the back of the hotel where the conference is being held. The closer I get to the conference room, the louder the voices I hear.

"And as Pastor Cole liked to say, be aware of what season you're in. There is a time for everything under the sun and recognize your season."

Every so often I am led to read the book of Ecclesiastes. The book can be real melancholy, especially when I used to read it with a fifth of Hennessey. Lately, I have been contemplating chapter three, that talks about seasons. I wonder if I have moved into a different season, and I haven't realized it. Maybe I'm in a season to be out of the problem-solving business.

As I walk along the back of the conference I notice that there are less than a thousand people in attendance. That is rather small for an international conference. Only a thousand people at an international conference means something's afoot. I see Pastor Bryant on the side of the stage, and I can tell he's distracted, but if he thinks that he's been having a long day, his day is about to get longer.

I don't get any of the ushers' attention until I start walking up toward the stage to where Pastor Bryant and the other ministers sit. An usher walks toward me and meets me midway down the aisle.

"Can I help you?" One of the ushers holds up his hands to prevent me from going any farther.

If I was a cop I would break the usher's wrist and keep moving. However, I realize a more subtle approach is required. I look beyond the usher's shoulder and make eye contact with Pastor Bryant. I mouth to him, "We need to talk."

Pastor Bryant gets up and walks down the side of the podium. As soon as he gets down, his armor bearers meet him, but Pastor Bryant waves them off. I join Pastor Bryant on the ground floor and walk alongside the conference toward the exit.

We walk down a long hallway that leads to the office he took me to the first time we met. I walk into the office after Pastor Bryant opens the door. He turns on a light to a quaint office with a minirefrigerator on the inside of it.

"You must have some information for me seeing that you're here," Pastor Bryant says as he opens the refrigerator door.

"Who is Demetrius?" I ask.

"I never heard of him. What does he have to do with this?"

Judging by his body language, I can tell that Pastor Bryant is telling the truth. He doesn't know Demetrius, which narrows the list of people who I suspect informed Demetrius about me.

"Is that what you came over here to ask? That's most disappointing, Minister Dungy. I was told that you can be quite resourceful."

I don't respond well to criticism, but there is a larger problem looming. "Let's just say that I met Demetrius last night, and he's not the kind of guy you would want to be alone with in a room."

"Really?" Pastor Bryant seems unfazed by my statement. Instead, he starts checking his cell phone, and, I assume, texting.

There is a glass crystal ball on the desk. It's the size of a baseball, and it appears to be a replica of the globe. I pick up the ball from the mantle and toss it in my hands a couple of times before I hurl it past Pastor Bryant's head, and it shatters against the wall.

"Are you out of your mind!"

"Are you out of *your* mind? There's a guy who threatened me less than a few hours after I met with Pastor Cole's kid, and you don't even know who he is?"

"I don't know him. What else do you want me to tell you? Pastor Cole started hanging around some shady characters, and I had to start distancing myself from him."

"And yet, here you are at the conference as if nothing has happened."

"He's still a brother in Christ. I don't have to agree with every move he makes, but I will stand by him. But that's not the point; the point is . . . I sent you to deliver a message to Elisha. What happened?"

I reach into my jacket pocket and remove the letter Bryant had originally given me. I toss it on the table. "Return to sender. She thought your offer was a joke. She wants double."

"Double?" Pastor Bryant shakes his head.

"Or she's going to expose the dirt that she has on you." I notice the change in Bryant's body position. He now knows just how good I am.

"What do you know?" Bryant asks.

"Not enough. I need to know what you are willing to pay $2 million for to keep from coming into the light."

"And why would I tell you that?"

"Because you're going to pay me two million to not only help find the person responsible for Cole's death, but to make sure that your secrets remain secret."

"Two million dollars? You've got to be kidding, Dungy. I'm not paying you $2 million."

"I'm putting my vacation on hold and my life is at risk. So if I'm going to do that, then I'm going to make sure that it's worth it. Two million dollars or I walk. It's really that simple."

Pastor Bryant mulls over my proposition. For me, it's a win-win situation. I either resume my much-needed vacation, or I'm about to get the ultimate payday.

"I can't believe I'm doing this," Bryant mumbles to himself. "You better deliver."

"I will. Not let's hear it. What does Elisha Davis have on you?"

"What do you know about the Cloth?'

I am somewhat surprised to hear Pastor Bryant mention "the Cloth" in a sentence.

"I know that they do not officially exist, but in certain circles they are an international conglomerate of pastors and religious leaders who share their resources together and big megachurches with Starbucks in the parking lot."

"That's not all that they do."

Obviously, but that is just a general assessment. I happen to know for a fact that the Cloth is also a safe haven for wayward pastors who need to indulge in some of their vices without causing a scandal. What I didn't know was that Pastor Bryant was somehow affiliated with it.

"How does Elisha know about the Cloth?"

"Because her father was a member of the Cloth as well," Bryant says.

I long suspected that Pastor Cole has a closet full of skeletons. Why does it seem like only in death a person's true nature comes out?

"So every leader that's here is a member of the Cloth?" I ask.

Bryant gives a head nod in agreement. "Well, not exactly. When I last saw Cole, he told me that he was getting out. After I found out about his death, I decided that when this conference is over, I'm getting out too."

Even though Pastor Cole believes his fellow members of the Cloth are above murder, the truth is, Pastor Cole's departure from the group, and then his murder, raises a lot of red flags.

"So what did Elisha catch you doing?"

Pastor Bryant lets out an embarrassed grin. "I was photographed in a hot tub with two women the other night. I don't know how she got that picture."

Neither do I. Elisha has turned out to be quite re-sourceful, but why would she have incriminating photos of an organization that her father was a part of? What did Elisha stand to gain? My face must've conveyed disap-pointment because Pastor Bryant gave me a dismissive wave.

"I didn't do anything, but it's pretty hard to resist being in a hot tub with two beautiful women."

"I'm sure that argument would go well with the wife."

Pastor Bryant gives a head nod to my sarcasm. I reach into my jacket pocket and pull out a small tablet with a pen. I scribble a number on the paper and hand it to Pastor Bryant. "Half now, half when the job is complete."

"What do you need from me?" Bryant says.

"I need a name with evidence and the photos."

Pastor Bryant purses his lips, but he then agrees. And just like that, I have become a millionaire.

Chapter Six

The next morning I find myself in attendance at New Haven Community Church. Like practically everything on the island, the church is a stone's throw away from the ocean. I kind of like having church close to the beach and being able to hear the sea while worshipping God.

The church could hold maybe sixty people at most. Less than thirty are in attendance, but, boy, I can feel the presence of God in this place. Adele invited Victory and me to church, and we sat in the front row clapping and singing along with the two-member praise team while Sammy Moses accompanies the praise team on piano.

"Bless that wonderful name of Jesus! Bless that wonderful name of Jesus!" the praise team sings.

I have to admit, Sammy is a pretty good piano player. He's not a Beethoven or a Thelonious Monk or even a Little Richard, but he does play the piano with enthusiasm. I enjoy watching him stare down at the keys as he thrusts his fingers down on the keyboard. The song went on for much longer than need be, but it is nice to see a church that thrives on praise as opposed to being theatrical.

"This feels like home. Look at Sammy get down," Victory says.

"That fool is going to mess around and hurt himself," Adele replies.

Sammy and Adele are both in their sixties, so I understand why Adele is concerned with Sammy's health and safety. She may not share a romantic connection with Sammy, but they do share the journey of getting older.

All of a sudden, Sammy stops playing and stands up. Now only the drums, tambourines, and hands clapping could be heard. Sammy walks up to the front of the stage and does a dance across it. Adele rolls her eyes at the sight of Sammy.

"He always got to show out."

Victory lets out a girlish laugh, and I smile. Even in the midst of Pastor Cole's murder, the mood in the sanctuary is not lost. I get the sense that there is still hope, and there is more life to live.

When the song concludes, Sammy walks off the stage and takes a seat next to Adele. He puts his arm around her, and she smoothly takes his arm off of her. Pastor Clayborn is a petite woman who is barely taller than the pulpit. She walks up with a Bible in her hands that is bigger than her.

"This has been a grievous week," Pastor Clayborn says in her raspy voice. "I have never met Pastor Cole. Like some of you, I was only able to view him from the TV, which is not the best way to view a man."

I can tell that Clayborn is an educated woman who is only concerned with one thing, and that is the truth.

"You see, man looks at a man subjectively; God looks at a man objectively. If a man is a man of faith but struggles with alcohol, then man will demonize him and call him an alcoholic. God sees both the man with a drinking problem and the promise that is birthed within him. He doesn't step away. No, he gets right into the thick of it and begins to reconcile and reshape and mold that man into his original purpose. Just like God is molding all of us to accomplish His will. Don't get too caught up in yourself to see that you're a part of something much greater in the body of Christ."

I know that I have struggled with drinking and smoking for a long time, to the point where I stop referring to myself as a man of God. I have troubles seeing a flawed man worthy of such a title. Pastor Clayborn reminds me of the power of God and His ability to transform lives. Maybe I am a man of God. A deeply flawed man of God, but a man of God, nonetheless.

After service, Pastor Clayborn stands outside on the side of the church. She doesn't rush through every member, but she takes her time and talks with each of them like she has known them for all of her life.

"Thank you, Pastor Clayborn, that was an awesome sermon," I say.

"Thanks, to God be the glory."

Just like that, my mind starts to turn and I wonder if Pastor Clayborn would carry that same humility in the States, where name brands are worshipped. I wonder if being on a secluded island helps one avoid temptation as opposed to living in an environment that embraces it and flaunts it.

"That was a great sermon, Pastor Clayborn."

I recognize the voice, and when I turn around, there he is . . . Demetrius. I know for a fact that Demetrius was not at service this morning. His large girth and sinister grin is easy to spot at a church. But how did he know I was here?

"God bless you," Pastor Clayborn says with a crooked smile. She obviously knows who Demetrius is and is not buying the sinner-coming-to-church gimmick.

"I seem to have forgotten your name," Demetrius says to me.

"Nic." I extend my hand, and Demetrius shakes it.

"God bless you, Brother Nic," he says.

I have a short list of things I hate. On that list is grapefruit, the 405 freeway, and nonbelievers who mock Christians. Demetrius is the latter.

"Nic, I was wondering if I could have a word with you in private."

Somehow, I don't think that this is a request. We are in public so there's not much he can do with a bunch of eyewitnesses, so I excuse myself from Pastor Clayborn and walk with Demetrius until we get out of earshot of others.

"Okay, I don't particularly like being messed with, so what's up?" I ask.

Demetrius acts like he is offended. "I'm shocked. I can't believe you would think that I would waste your time."

"Well, you wanted my attention, and you got it."

"I wanted to apologize for the other night. I know I can come on a little strong, but my intentions are good," Demetrius says.

"Did you ever hear the expression that the road to hell is paved with good intentions?" I ask.

Demetrius loses his smile. How easy it is for the serpent to shed his skin, and just like that . . . His smile returns.

"I never heard that expression before, Mr. Dungy, but I will keep that in mind."

I bet he will, but I'm still wondering why Demetrius has taken a sudden interest in me. The only way I will find out is by having a conversation with him.

"What do you want, Demetrius?"

"I was wondering if we could have a private conversation."

"What do you call this?" I ask.

"Two brothers in Christ having a conversation," Demetrius says.

"I didn't take you for a Christian."

Demetrius laughs, and he starts to look down at his feet. "I guess not, Mr. Dungy, but there is something time sensitive I need to talk to you about."

"I'm listening. What's on your mind?"

"Not here. Come to my house around ten p.m. It's the biggest house on the island."

Again, I suspect that this is not a request. "It's a date."

From church I hitch a ride with Sammy back to his house. My meeting with Demetrius gave me a lot to feel nervous about. As we drive along the road that leads to Sammy's house, I take in the scene. Sammy didn't have a big retirement to live off of, but who does in this day and age?

He bought his house in the part of Crystal Cove which is similar to a ghetto that I've seen back in the States. It's about a ten-minute drive from Adele's beach house. Ten minutes . . . That's all that separates a slum from a dream home.

"You okay, Doc?" Sammy asks.

I hear Sammy, but I don't respond. My attention is set on the people walking around these neighborhoods. There are young boys with their shirts off who are walking about aimlessly. The young girls are half-naked and clueless, but who am I to judge? Demetrius came up on these streets, so, in essence, he's only doing what these streets taught him.

"Doc, you've been acting goofy on me ever since that girl of yours came out here."

"I'm sorry, Sam. I just have had a lot on my mind."

"I know, and it hasn't been the right thing. You've been running back and forth to Green Cove and not communicating with folks. It looks bad, man."

I didn't have time to worry about how my actions look, especially when I have a drug dealer who has made threats on my life looking for me. And I have no reason to believe that Demetrius will not make good on his threats. I don't want anyone to get the wrong idea about me, but what can I do?

Sammy pulls into his driveway. Like most homes on the island, Sammy's place is only one story. I guess that's to protect against the storm season, though I could be wrong. Unlike the other homes in the neighborhood, Sammy takes pride in his home. The yard is kept up, and there isn't any trash or anything that would create an eyesore.

I follow Sammy into his home, and it's a different story. While the outside of the house is kept as immaculate as possible, the inside of the house looks like a category-three tornado hit it. Newspapers, fishing equipment, and empty bottles of beer are scattered all over the place.

"Would you like a cold one, Doc?" Sammy asks.

"Sure."

Sammy goes into his refrigerator and produces two domestic beers and pops the cap back on both of them.

Sammy isn't a heavy drinker. He enjoys a good beer, but he never drinks in front of someone who has struggles with alcohol. The Bible says, "Do not cause your brother to struggle." Of course, if Sammy knew about my struggle with alcohol, I doubt he would offer me a beer. I have always been somewhat delusional about my alcohol problem and not wanting to confide in Sammy about my struggles makes me question how genuine of a friend I am to him.

"So what's on your mind?" Sammy asks after he takes a swig of his beer.

"What's not on my mind? I can't even call it nowadays."

"Well you seem a little distraught since we left church."

"Demetrius showed up at church today," I say before I take a sip of my beer.

"I know. He ain't hard to miss. So what about Demetrius showing up at church?"

"He wants to meet with me."

For the first time, Sammy gives me a look of concern. He may not be so quick to demonize Demetrius like how Adele does; however, that doesn't mean that Sammy thinks Demetrius is an upstanding citizen either.

"Now why would he want to talk with you?"

This is the part where my friendship and my profession collide. I can't tell Sammy why Demetrius wants to meet with me, but I need his advice on what to do in this situation.

"I don't know, maybe he needs some spiritual counsel."

"Well, we all are in need of spiritual counsel. If Demetrius wants to turn his life around, then I say you should at least hear him out."

Something tells me that Demetrius is not interested in a "Come to Jesus meeting." "You may be right, Sam, but listen, since I don't know who I'm dealing with, I have to ask you, do you have a piece?"

"A peace? Yeah, I have a peace that surpasses all understanding."

"I'm not talking about that kind of peace. I'm talking about steel, heat—a gun."

Sammy takes a swig of his beer but does not swallow. He just looks at me. The moment turns awkward because Sammy's look is a look of disappointment. He finally swallows his beer.

"Now, why in the world would you need a gun?"

"I just don't want to find myself in a jam with this guy, and I don't have any protection."

"I thought the Holy Spirit is your protection," Sammy says.

"The Holy Spirit is my guide and my comforter, but what if Demetrius doesn't respect the Holy Spirit?"

"Don't matter. If Christ be lifted up, then He will draw all men to you. If you're lifting Him up, then you ain't got nothing to worry about. That is the question you have to ask yourself," Sammy says.

I wish it was that simple, and I wish that I didn't get myself mixed up in a situation where I would have to make such a dangerous request of Sammy. "I'm sorry, man, I'm just a little worried about meeting with him."

"You know you could cancel," Sammy says.

"That's not an option."

"I don't understand; why not?"

"It's just not. Trust me, I have to go."

Sammy takes another swig and sits there and stares at me. Growing up, I was in search of a father figure, and I found them in the church. My father was only in my life for a brief moment and in that time he caused more harm than good. Sammy is the first real father figure I have and to see him look at me with so much disappointment is a little too much for me to bear right now.

Sammy gets up and goes into his room, and for a few minutes all I hear is rumbling going on until Sammy reenters the living room with a .38 revolver in his hand.

"I'm going to loan you 'Old Bessie.' You bring her back now, you hear?"

This gun is perfect for robbing stagecoaches. I can both feel and see the rust on this gun as I hold it in my hands. In short, I've seen water guns that are more intimidating. "Did you steal this off of Jesse James?"

"She'll work just fine, but I have to admit, it's strange for a minister to feel like he has to carry a gun to preach the Gospel."

Strange indeed, but tonight, I'm not sure if it's going to be the Gospel that will be preached. "You know what, Sammy? That's okay. I'm going to take your advice and listen to the Holy Spirit."

"Now you're talking, Doc."

I just hope that it's the Holy Spirit and not my instincts telling me not to show up to this meeting empty-handed. I can't afford to make a mistake if this meeting with Demetrius goes south.

Chapter Seven

From Sammy's place, I go back to Adele's house. Adele is sitting in her living room with the TV on while reading a magazine.

"Hey, Adele."

"Hey, sugar. I was wondering where you were," she says.

"I hung out with Sammy for a minute. Where's Victory?"

"Victory is in her room taking a nap."

Adele gives me a look that reinforces the no shacking up in her house rule. I'm spending so much time hunting down a murderer that the thought of being tempted by a beautiful woman is the farthest thing on my mind.

"What's wrong with you?" Adele asks.

"Demetrius came by the church today."

"I know, I saw him there too. Even the devil goes to church sometimes."

"Yeah, he's starting to pop up everywhere I go, and it's making me nervous."

Adele lets out a grunt before she gets up and starts to head out of the living room. "Come on, I got something for you."

I follow Adele out of the living room, and we walk past one of her two bathrooms to the room that she has kept closed the entire time I've been here.

This is the one room that she does not rent out to guests. Adele opens the double doors, and it becomes clear why this room is off-limits.

The room is a memorial to Adele's late husband, Melvin Paige. In this room there are wedding photos, certificates of service, and Melvin's service uniform. Melvin served in the army during Vietnam. Something else, in this room are all of Melvin's weapons. Guns, knives, you name it. I'm sure that when he was alive, Adele felt safe.

"Here you go. You can use this." She hands me a 9 mm pistol.

I didn't expect for Adele to have this many guns in her house. I mean, I don't think anybody would be foolish enough to try to break into her home, but Adele is prepared if a small army invades her home.

"Thank you, Adele."

"It was Melvin's gun. I walked in one day and see him with that gun in his mouth. The war changed him."

"So I hear."

"Yeah, he went into himself and resented everybody and everything, including God. He was mad at God for what he had to do to survive."

"What did you do?" I ask.

"I did what came natural. I loved him through it. I prayed for him for years, and for years I thought that God wasn't listening. Then I had a revelation that God is eternal. He's not bound by time, but He does pay attention to position. Melvin had to be in the right position to forgive God, and he and I had to be in the right position to love Him unconditionally."

Adele's tale is both heartbreaking and cautionary. If Melvin could overcome his past to enjoy what he had with Adele, then why can't I? Perhaps there is still hope for me as long as I am willing to walk away from the things that are destroying me.

"Thanks again, Adele."

"No problem, sweetie. You take care of yourself."

"Will do." I take the gun and head upstairs to my room.

I get on the phone and call Paul from the *LA Times*. After several missed calls and several urgent text messages, Paul finally answers the phone.

"Even on vacation you're still a pain in the neck."

"Brother, it's good to hear from you." I mean it, I don't have very many friends, but Paul is one of them. "So you got that information for me?"

"I know you've been in the Bahamas, but out here, we have a really tight mayoral race, and I've been really busy."

The mayoral race is the furthest thing on my mind. I have an unknown enemy which is not good, because I don't know how to fight him. Paul's information can give me the advantage that I need.

"Yes, I got that information for you, and to sum it up, if you see this guy heading toward you, run in the opposite direction."

Now that we have established a firm grasp on the obvious, I need Paul to dig deeper. There has to be more that Paul is leaving out. "Lay it on me. What else did you find out?"

"He basically owns three-fourths of the island you're on, but a lot of it has been bought through shell companies. He even owns a chunk of the island that the pastor who was murdered was killed on."

Now that is both surprising and unsettling news. It doesn't take much to know that Demetrius is calling the shots around here, but the fact that he owns so much property on this island is disturbing because it means it's possible he may have something to do with Pastor Cole's death after all.

"Now the property he owns is very interesting. He owns the airport and three-fourths of the landing strip."

"How do you own three-fourths of a landing strip?"

"That is the original length of the landing strip, but the pilots were having trouble landing on it, and Demetrius refused to put up the money to extend the landing strip. Then comes in Randall Knott with his millions. He bought the land around the airport and extended the landing strip."

"I'm sure that didn't sit well with Demetrius."

"It didn't. He wasn't making money, but he didn't make a big fuss."

"Why not? That doesn't sound like the Demetrius I've met."

It is a fair question. A guy is losing money and business and nothing happens. That is curious, to say the least.

"If I have to guess, Demetrius is a drug dealer, and he uses that airport to run drugs and conduct all of his shady business dealings."

All I hear is drugs, and I check out. This adds a volatile piece to the puzzle—a drug runner, a business tycoon, and a dead preacher all on the same island. There are a million questions in between.

"This guy wants to meet me tonight."

"Tonight? Didn't you just *hear* what I just said? You *can't* be that stupid."

"I don't think I have a choice."

"You *do* have a choice. You can stop being stupid and come home."

"There are people whose lives will be at risk if I don't meet with him."

Paul doesn't respond. He doesn't wish me well; he just hangs up the phone. I'm sure he's disgusted with me at this point. His final warning to me is not to do anything stupid, but I seem prone to do stupid things.

Chapter Eight

One day, I'm going to do the right and smart thing. Tonight is not that night. It's 9:50 p.m. and in a few minutes, one of Demetrius's minions will pick me up. I don't know if I'll return from this meeting, but I know that I have to find out the truth. The search for truth has made me the man that I am today. I pray that this quest does not lead to my demise.

"Nic, you don't want any dessert?" Victory extends a slice of Adele's sinful lemon cake toward me.

"No, thanks, I have to go somewhere for a little bit."

"Where are you going at this hour? We have cake, and we're about to watch *Justified*."

"*Justified* doesn't come on tonight," I reply.

"I have four episodes recorded," Adele says from the other side of the kitchen.

As much as I would love nothing more than to sit and eat cake, I would love to even watch *Justified*, but something tells me that Demetrius is not someone who handles being stood up.

"I'll just be gone for a minute. I'll be back in a little bit." That is a lie. It's the second lie I've told Victory since I have met her; it's becoming a habit.

"Wait a minute, Nic. I thought that we were going to have a nice evening together where we spend quality time?"

"We will, I promise."

Victory cocks her head to the side, and I realize that I did something I shouldn't have done. I made her a promise, and the worst thing I can do is promise Victory something I can't fulfill.

"Okay. No problem. Have a nice meeting." Victory shrugs her shoulders and goes back into the kitchen.

I head for the door before I do something that I will regret . . . like not show up to this meeting. I had my sports coat on to conceal the gun Adele gave me earlier. I pray that I won't have to use it.

"Nic," Adele says.

I stop and turn to look at her. "Adele, I have to go."

"It'll just take a minute. We can step outside."

I step outside of the house, and Adele closes the door behind her. The clock is ticking, and I don't have time for a sermon.

"I know you have to go, but let me tell you that you're making a mistake."

"You're going to have to be a little more specific," I say, since at this point, there are a few mistakes that I'm making.

"That girl has come all the way out here for you. That's a special girl, but you know that already."

"I know. I know, and I'm trying."

"Knowing is one thing, applying is something different," Adele says.

"You're quoting Bruce Lee," I say.

"Child, hush. The point is, trying isn't enough, not for someone like Victory. Don't be a fool."

"I am a fool. I'm just hoping that one day I'll wise up."

In the end, all I can do is shrug my shoulders as I step away from Adele. I walk away from her house remembering the sad look on Victory's face and Adele's words etched in my mind. That look will haunt me. This is not the trip I had envisioned for us. I walk along the back of

Adele's house and at 10 p.m. on the dot, a Jeep pulls up. A window rolls down, and all I see is darkness; darkness and a man's face that I can't make out.

"Get in."

That's all he says.

"Right to business, I like that," I say.

I get into the car and not another word is said between my mystery driver and me. We travel up one long, winding road that leads to the top of the hill where Demetrius's house is located. In a place of paradise, Demetrius rules as king. I can say one thing for sure: when it gets dark on the island, it get terrifyingly dark. I realize I take things like streetlights for granted.

We arrive at the top of the hill, and the driver turns off the engine and exits the car without another word. I know why I'm here, so there's no need for further instructions. I just start walking toward Demetrius's mansion.

For a drug lord, the security is pretty nonexistent. Either Demetrius is low on the criminal totem pole, or no one is stupid enough to try anything. I don't think either scenario plays well for me, but I do lean more toward the former as opposed to the latter. I follow the driver through the front door.

Once inside, it's all-black. I can't even begin to make out the interior except for the golden chandelier and the bright light that radiates from the living room. Once in the living room, I see the biggest projection screen I have ever seen in my life. A soccer match is on. One of Demetrius's henchmen proceeds to conduct a search. He pats me down and finds the gun Adele gave me in my back pocket. He takes the gun and walks over to Demetrius.

"He had this on him," the henchman says as he hands the gun over to Demetrius.

Now that Demetrius knows that I'm carrying, this meeting can get real interesting. I just hope that it doesn't turn deadly.

"You brought a gun to a meeting? How Christian of you," Demetrius says.

"Most Christians I know carry heat. They cling to the Old Testament," I say.

Demetrius laughs, and even some of his henchmen manage to chuckle. The gun turned out to be a stupid play, but it got a laugh out of Demetrius, which kills the tension in the room.

"Do you like soccer, Mr. Dungy?" Demetrius says with his back to me while sitting on the couch and smoking a cigar.

"It's okay." In truth, the only things that I know about soccer is that it's a bore to watch compared to football, and that David Beckham used to be a great player. Now he is just an underwear model.

The thing I find most alarming about Demetrius is that he knows my name, which means he's resourceful. They are a real chatty group. It's clear that Demetrius rules over his men with fear. I need to gauge where Demetrius is mentally, and while I think this move is stupid, I doubt that it could be any more stupid than me getting into the car with a loaded gun.

"So are we going to do this or what?"

"What?" Demetrius says as he sits up and turns toward me.

"Well, seeing that you had no problems killing one preacher, I'm sure you won't hesitate to kill another."

Yeah, I'm sure that was a stupid move. Demetrius stood up and walks toward me. He is, without a doubt, one of the most imposing individuals I've met. He dwarfs me. I wouldn't stand a chance in a fair fight. I give Demetrius a once-over. I'm looking for weak points, but I can't find any. He just stares at me without a shirt on, and with Demetrius's dark skin, the ink of his tattoos are barely recognizable considering.

"You think I brought you here to kill you? Is *that* why you brought a gun?" Demetrius looks surprised.

"I certainly don't think you brought me here for prayer. So let's get on to the reason why I'm here, because it's getting past my bedtime."

Demetrius gives me an evil smirk. Boy, I wish I could wipe that smirk off his face.

"Why would I want to kill a preacher?"

"My guess, he found out something about you that you didn't want anybody to know," I say.

Demetrius nods his head as he takes another puff on his cigar. I can't even begin to draw the connection between Demetrius and Pastor Cole, but there must be a connection there somewhere.

"I didn't kill that preacher. I don't know how you do things in the States, but where I'm from, it's disrespectful for a man to accuse another man of something in his own home."

The smirk is gone. Now Mr. Hyde has stepped in. Now it's time to dance.

"Threaten a man and those who he cares about are disrespectful in any country," I say.

I need to show him that I'm not afraid . . . even though I am terrified. Demetrius can kill me just like he may have killed Pastor Cole. Only difference is while Pastor Cole's murder caused a small ripple, my death won't cause any ripple at all. Many would rejoice over my death, and only a few would mourn. I imagine Paul would, Spider, Victory, Adele, and Sammy, but that's it. The road of a fixer is a lonely road, and it has to be if a fixer is worth his salt.

In a sudden twist, Demetrius starts to laugh. Neither one of us cracked a joke. One thing I can tell from Demetrius's laugh is that he didn't bring me here to kill me. He would've done it already. No, Demetrius brought me here to use me, but in what capacity I'm not sure.

"Why are you not with the rest of them?"

"The rest of them—you mean the ministers at the conference on the island next door?"

Demetrius gives me a head nod. Now I know that part of this meeting is about what's going on at Green Cove.

"I didn't come here for the conference. I'm on vacation. Plus, I don't play well with others," I say.

"Finally, something we both have in common," Demetrius says.

In the future, I'm going to try to avoid having too many things in common with a drug lord.

"You spend your vacation poking your nose in other people's affairs?" Demetrius asks.

My knee-jerk reaction is no, but if I take an objective view of the past few days, then even I would have to conclude that I have spent more time in other folks' business than actually enjoying the sun.

"I did mention it's my bedtime?" I ask.

"All right, then, I'll get to the point. You've been utilizing my airport a lot since you've been here."

"I thought the airport belongs to Randall Knott," I say just to stir the pot.

"It's *my* airport," Demetrius's voice reverberates throughout the room like thunder.

I knew that, but playing devil's advocate allows me to better gauge from what angle Demetrius is coming from. It also allows me to see just how much animosity Demetrius has toward Knott. Is it enough to make him want to kill everyone and everything in his path?

"It's my airport. I own the landing strip that you land on. Randall Knott is a thief. Any man associated with him is a thief as well. So what does that make you, Mr. Dungy?"

"I couldn't care less about Randall Knott, and I really don't care about the dead preacher so long as killing preachers doesn't become a habit," I say.

Demetrius lets out a monstrous laugh. It gives me the chills; his voice sounds like he has something demonic on the inside of him. Maybe it's my mind, or maybe Demetrius is demon-possessed, which would explain a lot of things.

"Well, I may not be a God-fearing man, but I don't kill preachers. Of course, there is always that exception. You may have to ask Knott."

"Why would I ask him?"

"Because there wasn't any dead preachers until he got involved. They've had their conferences for years, no problems. Then all of sudden, this year, there's bloodshed."

I hate to admit this, but part of me believes him. He doesn't have a reason to lie to me. He could bury me somewhere on this island where no one will be able to find me and not lose an ounce of sleep. Demetrius confessing to me that he didn't kill Cole means that there is something he needs from me.

"I'll make sure to ask Knott, but what's the point of me being here?"

"Two things. One, the girl you visited yesterday, don't ever go to her house again."

"Why is that?" I ask.

"I'm a friend that doesn't want her to be bothered."

That means Elisha has a connection with Demetrius, which means that Demetrius didn't kill her father. I'm back at square one with no real leads. Tomorrow, I'm going to have to go back to Elisha's place and deliver the check from Pastor Bryant to her.

"What's the second thing?"

"The second thing is since you're a minister and Knott can't tell the difference between one preacher and another, I want you to find out what he's planning, and then report back to me."

"So I work for you now?"

"God, no. Work would imply that I'm going to pay you. No, this is a favor."

"A favor? A favor will imply that you will owe me one, then," I say.

Demetrius puts his cigar out in a nearby ashtray. He still has plenty of cigar left. Either he's wasteful or he put out the cigar to illustrate a point.

"You find out what I need to know and I won't stop by Adele's house for some of her coconut cake. Which, I hear, is quite good."

I will never forgive myself for getting Adele involved in my mess. I have a home, and I can get up and go back at a moment's notice. Adele, on the other hand, has to stay on the island with this monster.

There are not too many ways I can play this, and I can't negotiate from a position of weakness. I have to convince Demetrius that I have the upper hand, when, in actuality, I don't.

"I don't think you would want to show up at Adele's house uninvited, and you don't have to make threats to convince me to help you. Threats are usually made by someone who doesn't have power."

Demetrius takes a step closer. He is now in striking distance, but I doubt there is anything I could do that would even stun a behemoth like him. Physically, I'm powerless.

"You'd be even more of a fool if you think that I don't have power."

"You don't, because if you did, you would know what Randall Knott has planned, but you don't," I say.

"You're just a big-time gangster on a small island. You're no match for someone like Randall Knott who can crush you without leaving his breakfast table. You don't want me to spy on Knott for you; you need me too."

After my last comment, I took a deep breath and braced for Demetrius to plummet me. He balled up his fist and even looked like he was going to do it, but he didn't. Instead, he swallowed his anger and let his smile take over.

"I like you, Nic. You got guts, I'll give you that. You're right, I do need you, but I don't need Adele or that old man or that sweet girl that you've been walking around with. So what's it going to be?"

I love how he frames that question . . . as if I have a choice in the matter. I don't. Tomorrow I would have to go knocking on Randall Knott's door to see what I can find out about Pastor Cole's death. As far as Demetrius's first request goes, after I deliver the money to Elisha, we can go our separate ways.

"I'll look into it," I say.

"As they say, pleasure doing business with you." Demetrius extends his arm to the front door.

"You really should watch soccer," he says just before I reach the door. I turn to look at him. "It's a game of strategy and endurance."

Strategy and endurance. Those are the two things I'll need if I'm going to survive this ordeal.

"I'll keep that in mind." I then head out the door.

"Don't forget this." Demetrius summons one of his henchmen to bring me my gun.

He takes the gun and examines it with a smile before handing it over to me. "Here, the gun is a little too girly for my taste."

Demetrius lets out a big laugh, and the other men join in on the laugh. Well, at least I got Adele's gun back, and I didn't have to use it.

My driver walks beside me and escorts me back to the car. A deal has just been concluded, but I wonder which devil I made it with.

Chapter Nine

For the first time since we met, I'm trying to avoid Victory. I can't handle her disappointment in me. I can't bear entering the room and seeing this woman who I care about being so disgusted to even look at me. What is even more frustrating is that I'm being played by two men. I have allowed myself to be played, which is even more frustrating. Two men are using me as a pawn—Pastor Bryant and Demetrius—to do their bidding, and then there is Knott. I haven't met him, but I'm certain that he will want to employ my services as soon as we meet. Provided that I get close enough to Mr. Fortune 500 to even have a conversation with him.

I wouldn't blame Victory for wanting to pack up her things and leave. I'm sure this is not the trip she had in mind. That's the reason why I don't let anyone get close. That's the reason why I'm alone. I can't tear myself away from the problem-solving business, and I'm afraid of the man I would be without it. I thought Victory would be different. I mean, I thought that I would be a different person with her. We have a connection, and there's no denying it, but it seems like as strong as the connection we have, the pull to my dark calling is stronger. Lord knows where I will end up when this song plays out. Maybe it will end with me being in the lake of fire.

I finally found enough intestinal fortitude to get up and head downstairs. As I get closer to the kitchen I can smell the biscuits being made. Adele makes her biscuits from scratch. I arrive at the kitchen where, at the end of Adele's long white table, sits Victory. She's cutting up a mango.

"I'll be ready for you in a minute, sugar," Adele says to Victory.

"Okay," Victory says before she turns to me and flashes me a smile.

The smile is neither pleasant nor condemning; it just conveys that she's content. That means she still hasn't given up on me, and it's up to me to turn things around.

"Did you sleep okay?" Victory asks me, but she doesn't make eye contact.

"Yeah, I slept fine."

In truth, I didn't sleep. I can't sleep. The lives of those who I care about are at stake, and I have millions of reason why I need to find out who killed Pastor Cole. Sleep doesn't come to a man that has a million questions weighing on his head.

"Nic, could you set the table?" Adele asks.

"Sure."

I take the plates and the silverware from her and walk outside onto her deck and start to set the table.

Victory comes outside. She still avoids eye contact. She starts to place fruit and biscuits in the center of the table.

"About last night," I say, but Victory stops me with her hand.

"Last night was last night. Let's just have breakfast and go on with our day."

My mission is taking its toll on the serene personality of Victory. That is the last thing I want, but I had to go last night to ensure her safety.

Of course, I can always return Pastor Bryant's money and spend the rest of my time here with Victory.

We ate a nice breakfast and made small talk. After breakfast, Victory and I decide to help Adele by doing the dishes together.

"I want to take you somewhere," I say.

"Really? You sure you want me to tag along?"

I feel the sting of that dig. I deserve it, and in all honesty, I deserve way worse than what Victory is giving me.

"Yes, you and only you, but it's a little bit of a hike."

Victory flashes a smile, and it's a pleasant one. "You're tired of getting whooped in swimming, I see."

I throw my hands up in mock surrender. "You got me there. I am tired."

"Okay. I'll go easy on you and give you a break from the butt-whooping," she says.

Behind Adele's home is not only a road, but on the other side of the road there is a narrow trail. A trail the tropical trees overlap and provide shade for, but there is still enough space where the sun can break through. Victory and I walk side by side along this narrow trail. The path is so narrow that sometimes I would walk in front of Victory.

"Has Adele taken you along this trail?"

"No, Sammy told me about this trail, and I decided to walk it one day. I thought about you when I arrived at this one spot."

"Really?"

"Really," I say.

"Well, that makes a girl feel special."

I look back, and there is Victory's smile again. Her smile is a gift to me, and I would give anything for that smile to remain permanently on her face, maybe even a million dollars. She takes out her cell phone and starts to snap pictures. Then she catches me looking at her with one raised eyebrow.

"What? This is proof that I was here."

"You haven't seen nothing yet. You may want to save those pictures for later."

We keep on walking until the road widens and we're able to walk side by side. Victory takes my hand and walks with me. She seems to have forgiven me for my transgressions, which is amazing in itself. I don't know any women who can handle being invited to paradise by a man, and that man being gone half the time. Of course, Victory is unlike any woman I've ever met.

I came to a sudden stop and motioned for Victory to stop as well.

"What is it?" she asks.

I don't respond to her verbally, I just signal for her to listen with her ears.

I point up, and at the very top of the tropical tree, we can hear the sound of birds as they race from one tree to the next. It's a beautiful sound, one that I can't put into words; I can only show it to Victory. We are only halfway to our destination, but when Mother Nature is putting on such a wonderful display, we can't help but to sit and listen. Victory lets out a playful laugh.

"I love Sac, but this is breathtaking."

Victory takes another picture on her cell phone.

"You still haven't seen nothing yet." I extend my hand, and Victory takes it, and we continue our journey.

"You keep saying that. I hope I'm not being built up for a disappointment," she says.

"No, you're not. Believe me, it will be worth it."

We continue walking, and the road narrows, and Victory starts to walk behind me once again.

"Where did you go last night?"

It's naïve for me to think that a long walk in paradise would avoid Victory's obvious question.

"I had a meeting with someone that I couldn't miss."

"At ten o'clock at night? What kind of meeting?"

"I can't really get into it."

"There are a lot of things that you don't talk about and I wonder why."

I don't want to lie to Victory, but can she really handle me telling her that I spent last night with a drug lord who threatened me and those close to me?

"You know, it took an act of faith for me to get on the plane and come here. I wish you would show me the same kind of faith."

"What do you want to know?"

"I want to know you, but it seems like your work in the ministry overshadows you as a person."

"Oftentimes, I can't tell the difference."

"No, there's more to you, Minister Dungy, than the ministry. There's more to you. Your title doesn't make you; it only illuminates the man that you are."

Maybe there is, but it's buried deep down, and I lack the strength to excavate my true nature. Even now, surrounded by this beauty and with this beautiful woman, I can't pull myself away from the mystery surrounding Pastor Cole's death. Yesterday, I was certain that Demetrius was the killer, but now it looks like it may be Randall Knott, and that's a much-tougher man to get to than Demetrius.

"And whenever I ask you a personal question, you seem to space out on me like you're doing just now."

"I'm sorry. I have a lot on my mind."

"Be present."

"I'm trying."

"You're thinking being in the moment is not about thinking. If you're trying to be in the moment, then you'll never get there. Being in the moment means you don't think about anything else; you just experience what's in the here and now."

That's a dangerous way to live . . . in the moment. I'm afraid of who I am if I just let go and live in the moment. I'm afraid of what my urges would do if I gave them free reign. No, for a minister, even one that is not so straitlaced, the moment can be very threatening.

We arrive at the spot that I want to show Victory. There is a little river that has a small waterfall next to it. I have seen beauty since coming to this island, but this place that is deep in the tropical forest provides me with serenity.

"This is it? This is the place you've been trying to show me?" Victory asks.

I detect a hint of disappointment in her voice.

"Yeah, this is it," I say as I relieve myself of the picnic basket I had over my shoulder. "Sorry to disappoint."

"No, I'm just curious as to how you found out about this place? It's not exactly a hop, skip, and a jump away."

"No, it's not. I discovered this trail about the second day here. I started walking on this trail, and I kept walking until I arrived here."

I motion to the waterfall. I start to unwrap the blanket and lay it down over the dirt ground. I didn't have a clue about what I was doing.

"And what did you think about with me?" Victory asks.

"I wonder what you would think of this place. I wonder if I would ever get a chance to share this spot with you."

"Well, my coworkers think that I'm crazy for flying out here on the whim."

"A leap of faith like you said," I say.

"Yeah, that's what I told them. They are living vicariously through me. They expect to hear stories of romance and adventure when I get back."

More like tales of murder, mayhem, a drug dealer, and coconut cake.

Victory sits down on the blanket, and I take a seat next to her. We share mangos, papaya, and other fruits I packed away for the trip, along with water and some fresh Bahamian Johnny bread that Adele baked. For a long time we eat in silence and enjoy the view and the sound the birds made as they fly across the water. The moment was not without annoyance. Some of the bugs decide to buzz around my ear and use it for target practice, and I would occasionally have to swipe them away.

"So when do you plan to go back?" Victory asks.

"I don't know. I try not to think about going back."

"You know that there's this holiday coming up called Christmas. It's kind of a big deal in the church and the States."

Aside from the obvious that Christmas is a day the church decides to recognize the birth of Christ, Christmas carries very little value to me. It's too commercialized, too materialistic, and I have no tolerance for my Lord and Savior's day being reduced to Macy's sales and Black Friday deals.

"I hear the islands are beautiful around this time of the year. I thought about staying."

"I can imagine that these islanders would probably have a ball. Plus, who can resist the weather?"

"I don't know. Things are a lot simpler out here than back in the States," I say, with the exception of the fact that there is a murderer running between these two islands. Of course, I probably would be bored right now if it wasn't for the murder and Victory's surprise arrival.

"Well, my home would love to have you visit for the holiday."

Aside from the island, Victory's home is one of the few places I would rather be. Both places have given me a sense of family and connection. That means a lot to a loner like me.

"What's that over there?" Victory points to a small shack that is adjacent to the waterfall.

It was a shack that barely holds together, but considering the picturesque view that surrounds the hut, one would inquire as to the home's origins.

"There is a legend Sammy told about surrounding this house." I reach into a basket and grab a piece of bread. I break it in half and hand half to Victory. "The legend has it that during slavery, there was a ship that docked on this island. The slaves on the ship had an uprising, but were quickly dealt with; however, one slave managed to escape in the jungle. The owners searched for him for days and couldn't find him. Finally, they had to count their losses and sail on."

I point to the house. "That is supposedly the house that he built and lived in for the remainder of his days."

"Wow! Powerful. I'm surprised the hurricanes haven't destroyed it," Victory says.

"They have, but someone always manages to rebuild it. I guess it serves as a reminder that one can always change their fate."

"That's a lesson that still teaches us to this day," Victory says.

"Amen to that," I say.

"Amen," Victory says.

Amen indeed. Maybe I can change my fate as well. Become someone different, aspire to a higher calling.

Chapter Ten

All roads lead to Randall Knott. It's a no-brainer at this point, but before I can make a case for why one of the wealthiest men in the world would kill Pastor Cole, I have to establish a why. Why would Knott want to kill Cole? He has both the money and the influence, but there is one connection that Knott money and power hasn't reached, at least I don't think he has reached her.

Once again, I find myself outside of Elisha's house in spite of the fact that I was just warned by Demetrius to never go over to her place again. Of course, I've never been one to listen to authority, and if a conversation with Elisha can put this whole case to bed, then it's worth the risk. Plus, I have her $2 million check waiting for her.

"I hope you have good news for me," Elisha says after she opens the door and leaves it open for me to enter.

I close the door behind me to make sure we are alone. Discretion is still key; plus, I am suspicious that my moves are being watched, though I don't know who is watching me.

"You mean this?" I reach into my pocket and reveal an envelope that Pastor Bryant gave me. "Yes, but that's not all I have."

"Are you leaving, because that would be a great idea?"

I chuckle and wish that all I have to do is deliver a check filled with zeros. But I have another pressing matter to consider.

"I believe you have something to give to me," I say.

"I'll be right back." Elisha gets up and goes into her bedroom. Moments later, she comes back with an envelope of her own and hands it to me.

"Tell your preacher friend he needs to be more careful."

I take a look inside, and sure enough, these are photographs of Pastor Bryant in a precarious situation. "How did you come up with these?"

"My girlfriend was at the party they threw after the first night of the conference. She thought that it would be funny. Not to worry though. I had her send the pictures to my phone, and then delete them out of her phone."

"And I'm supposed to take your word for it that these are the only pictures floating around?" I ask.

"Why would you not believe me?"

"Your father was murdered, and I have yet to see you shed either a single tear or a concern about your safety. Now, I'm wondering why that is."

"How do you know that I don't cry?" Elisha asks with all of her feistiness.

"I don't know, but I doubt many know what you do behind closed doors."

"What I do behind closed doors would make you blush, Preacher." Elisha smiles and raises one eyebrow.

"I doubt it." I give her my own raised eyebrow.

"Well, ain't you full of surprises," she laughs.

"So did any of your father's words of wisdom rub off on you?"

Elisha picks up the check and examines it. She then shakes her head. "Not really. It's hard to listen to a man talk about God who wants your identity kept a secret."

"Your father obviously wasn't perfect. He was just trying to point you in the direction to someone who is."

"You're defending him now? You expressed that you didn't care too much for my father. Why the sudden change?"

"We had fundamental differences, as I said before, but nothing malicious. I just couldn't buy into his brand of doctrine."

"Well, many people shared the same feelings you had toward my father, and more. Some would even send death threats," Elisha says.

"Death threats? He told you about them?"

A clearer picture is starting to come into view between Pastor Cole and Elisha. I reckon every man needs one woman to be vulnerable to in his life. It might as well be a daughter that the majority of the world doesn't even know about, who just so happens to live on a small island.

"My father believed in never letting your enemies see you bleed. 'You save your tears and your fears for when you're in private, Elisha.' That's what he used to say."

Elisha fights back the tears and lets out a smile instead. Even now, she doesn't want to disappoint her father.

"I now know why you haven't cried before me."

Elisha picks up the check again in disbelief. One minute you are a bastard child that only a few people know about; the next minute you're a millionaire.

"Are you afraid to be walking around with that kind of money?" I ask.

"Like I said, no one is stupid enough to try something."

"Is it because of your affiliation with the local crime lord?"

Elisha is amused by my statement and knows who I am referring to. I just hope that Demetrius doesn't decide to pay me a visit after this meeting.

"You know a little too much to be a foreigner."

"You hang around with dangerous men."

"All men are dangerous, Mr. Dungy, especially a man who fancies himself as a preacher."

I detect a hint of seduction in Elisha's voice. She certainly was not daddy's little girl. This is why I came over here, because whether Elisha is a major player in this game remains to be seen, but I know that she knows more than she let on.

"I would love to hear this story," I say.

"It's not a very interesting one. It's just a classic tale of a good girl who's attracted to bad boys."

"I take it your father didn't approve?"

"My father didn't want to get in a disapproval contest."

I guess she's right. Pastor Cole has a lot more skeletons in his closet than his apparent daughter. One of those skeletons led to his demise.

"You need to be careful around men like Demetrius. He seems to be very protective of you, and that usually means that he's also controlling."

Elisha lets out a laugh like I had just made a joke. The arrogance of youth. I can never understand it.

"You laugh, but I bet Demetrius doesn't know about your newfound wealth."

"Of course not. He and I may have fun, but that doesn't mean I trust him," Elisha says.

"From what I've seen, Demetrius strikes me as a person who gets what he wants," I say.

"Demetrius may control a lot of people, but I'm not one of them."

"Does he know that?"

"You're a lot more fun today."

"Oh, I'm a blast to be around, but what I'm curious about is what your father had to do with Randall Knott."

"How would I know?"

"You seem to be pretty good about keeping secrets."

Elisha leans back on the couch and analyzes the check she just received. She can start a new life anywhere with that money.

"My father told me a lot of things; some things I am even embarrassed to repeat, but about Randall Knott, he didn't tell me anything."

"He didn't tell you anything at all? Not even on his last visit?" I find that strange.

Elisha tosses the check onto her coffee table as if it was a random bill and not a check worth $2 million.

"He did say how this would be the last time he would come to the conference. He wanted to make other arrangements to see me. But he didn't specify why."

It's not much, but Elisha's information is enough for me to know that I am at least heading in the right direction. Whatever business dealings Cole had with Knott, they must've fractured during this conference.

"You might want to ask Bishop Jackson," Elisha says.

"And why would I want to ask Bishop Jackson?"

"Because he and my father were thick as thieves."

I didn't even know Bishop Jackson is on the island. I didn't see him the other day. More importantly, I didn't even know that Pastor Cole and Bishop Jackson ran together, and I know just about every piece of church news and gossip.

"I thought your father and Pastor Bryant were close, seeing that Pastor Bryant just wrote you a rather large check."

"On the surface, yes, they were, but when it comes to doing dirt and someone who you can trust, that would be Bishop Jackson. That's who you would want to talk to."

I now know who the next person is that I will visit. I have to pay Pastor Jackson a visit and break this case wide open. I get up and head toward the door, but I stop right before I open it.

"One last question," I say.

"Yes, Mr. Preacher Man, what is it?"

"What now? You can go anywhere you want in the world."

"Do all Americans hate their current lives so much that they have to leave them as soon as they get money?"

"No, but with that money, you do have more options than before."

Elisha turns her head and appears to stare off into space. My question must have given her a chance to consider things that she has never considered before.

"How's Paris this time of the year?" Elisha asks.

"Cold, but it's still Paris."

"I'll keep that in mind when I grow tired of the warm weather," she says.

I smile and shake my head as I leave. If Elisha knows what's best for her, she would book a flight right away because things are about to heat up around here.

Chapter Eleven

It's around one o'clock in the morning when the phone rings, and it brings me out of my sleep. It takes a moment for my heart rate to settle down. I've been on edge a lot lately. I hope my cell hasn't woken up anyone else in the house. I take a look at the caller ID screen. It's Paul.

"What's up?" I say still half-asleep.

"Well, you called me needing information on Bishop Jackson, and I got something for you."

Information on the island is scarce, and I'm not at home where I have access to all of my resources. I need Paul to get as much info as possible on Bishop Jackson. I have never had him as a client, but Bishop Jackson is notorious for saying things that are not pulpit appropriate.

"What do you have for me?"

"Not much that didn't make it to the papers. I'll e-mail you what I got. You can do with it whatever you want," Paul says.

I'm thankful that Adele has Internet service, though it moves at a horse-and-buggy pace. I'll suffer through the service tomorrow as I print out Paul's e-mail.

"What else you got because you wouldn't call me unless you got something for me?"

"What do you know about Knott Corp. operations in Miami?" Paul asks.

"Very little, why?"

"Well, some unconfirmed sources say that Knott Corp. has taken some interest in the Bahamas, and they are seeking to purchase."

That is interesting news to find out, though not surprising. I know Knott has a vested interest in the Bahamas, but I'm not sure of what or why.

I get up and walk out onto the terrace where my room is located. There's a table there, and on it is my pack of cigarettes and my lighter. I light my cigarette and release a smoke trail into the air.

"I'm spit balling here, but there may be a connection between Knott business dealings and Pastor Cole."

"You may be right."

I already knew this, but there may be something more that Pastor Cole was entangled in with Knott.

"Who are you talking to?"

I turn around and see Victory standing in the doorway.

"Let me call you back," I say to Paul.

"Please don't," Paul says sarcastically, and then hangs up the phone.

I hang up the phone and put out my cigarette. "I was talking to a friend."

"You smoke?" Victory asks.

I take a look at the cigarette that I just put out. I don't really have anything to say. "Occasionally."

"Nic, we need to have a real honest conversation."

Victory walks in and has a seat on the miniature couch. I have a feeling that I'm not going to like this conversation, but this is a conversation that I can't avoid.

"What is going on with you?" she asks.

"I'm sorry about the smoking. I enjoy an occasional cigarette every now and then."

Victory starts to shake her head. "I don't even know if I believe a word that you are saying right now. Do you drink?"

Now I know how my clients feel. Victory's line of questioning is making me feel uncomfortable. I want to tell the truth, but the truth is ugly, and I would prefer to tell Victory a beautiful lie.

"I've struggled with drinking. It's not something I'm proud of," I say.

Victory gets up and begins to pace the floor. "Lord Jesus. This *always* happens to me."

I don't know much about Victory's past. We have only scratched the surface with each other, but at this moment, both of our pasts are starting to rise up.

"When were you planning to tell me?"

"I wasn't."

"You weren't? You weren't going to tell me?"

"No."

Victory puts her hands on her head unable to fathom the words that I'm saying to her right now.

"I was hoping that you would never have to see this, that I would have been delivered and spare you any pain."

"Am I that superficial? Do you think I can only handle certain parts of you?" Victory asks.

"Most people can't."

"I consider myself a patient woman. I'm neither insecure nor jealous. I know my worth and my value, but the one thing I can't handle is being lied to."

"I know, and I'm sorry," I say.

"I've had my dark moments as well, and I know about addictions."

"I'm sorry, I know this hasn't been the trip you had in mind but—"

Victory gives me a dismissive wave. She is through with the excuses and the lies. I can't blame her.

"Aside from the drinking and smoking, you have been in and out late at night and meeting with people who you can't talk about, which is amazing because from what I gather, this is your first time even visiting Crystal Cove. So I want you to be truthful, and I swear I can handle it. Who have you been seeing?"

"I don't understand."

"Nic, we're not exclusive. I don't know what we are, but now is the time to be honest and straightforward with me about what you are doing."

I can see how my dealing with Elisha and my late-night meeting with Demetrius can create a narrative that there's someone else who I'm seeing, but there isn't. All there is Victory. But what do I tell her? Do I tell her that I'm a church fixer, and the reason why I was in Sacramento a month ago was because her pastor's husband was missing? Do I tell her that a good portion of the pastors she respects and admires are former clients? Am I violating my clients' confidence by telling Victory the truth? Does it matter since if I resolve this issue, I plan to leave the game for good?

"You're doing that thing again where you don't respond, you just go into deep thought," Victory says.

"I haven't been completely honest with you."

"You have a firm grasp on the obvious."

"I'm not seeing anyone. I am trying to uncover the mystery surrounding Pastor Cole's murder."

"Are you a cop?"

I chuckle and shake my head. I'm not sure what I am anymore. "No, I'm not a cop; I'm what you call a 'fixer.'"

"A fixer? I didn't know people like that really exist. Well, except maybe in politics. How does one become a fixer?"

"That's a long story that I will tell one day, but I can say it starts with trying to help, and then it geos south really quick."

"So when we met in Sacramento, my pastor was one of your clients?"

"I can't disclose why I was in Sacramento. What I can tell you is that not in a million years did I expect to meet someone like you, and I've made it a rule not to get close, but you came into my life and shattered all of my rules."

Victory does a slight cock of her head to the side with a smile. "I've been known to do that."

At this moment, I don't think there is a strong enough word to describe what I'm feeling. There's something more I feel for her. I think I know what it is, but I'm terrified to say it. Saying that four-lettered word is dangerous because it makes me vulnerable, and I can't do what I do when I'm vulnerable.

"But this is different than fixing a problem at the church. This is dangerous. I mean, do you think the murderer is still on the island?"

"It's possible, but not to worry. I'm not trying to catch the killer. I just want to supply my employer with some information that can help him find the killer."

"That's what a detective does. Maybe you should let them do their job."

"I wish we lived in a world where the authorities cared about what happens in the church. Sadly, the police will probably declare this a cold case so that they can go on to more pressing issues."

The way Victory contorts her face, I can tell she is turning over in her mind my conundrum. "Okay, well, then, if you must continue to go down this road, I want to help."

"Victory, you can't. It can be dangerous."

"If it's too much for me, then I will say it's too much."

This is crazy to even consider it, but what choice do I have? "Okay, but you have to listen to me."

Victory gives me a head nod in agreement, but I doubt she knows what she just agreed to. "I will follow your lead," she says as she takes a seat on the couch, and I sit next to her.

"Addictions . . . What do you know about addiction?" I ask.

"In high school, I had a real bad addiction to smoking weed."

"In high school?"

"Okay, maybe college." She looks at me and sees that I'm not buying her story.

"Okay, until my late twenties, but then I found Jesus."

We cap off our night with a laugh, and I couldn't think of a better way to end it.

Victory, Sammy, and I arrive at the airport, and it looks like Donny Moses has some company. He's surrounded by three thugs.

"Looky, looky here," Sammy Moses says as he pulls up.

From a distance, I can tell that Donny Moses isn't intimidated by the thugs, even when one of them pulled out a knife that was visible from a distance.

"We should help him," I say . . . and everyone is silent.

I don't hear any response, and I'm on the verge of losing my nerve, so I get out of the car and start to walk toward Donny.

I look back, and it seems like Sammy is reluctant to get out and help his own son until Victory literally kicks him out the car. Sam gets off the ground and walks toward his son alongside me.

"What's the play?" Sammy asks.

"I have no idea."

We arrive and have the full attention of the three thugs.

"What business do you have here?" the guy with the long knife in his hands says.

"The business is that he's my pilot, and you are holding me up."

Everyone, Donny included, looks at me in a stupor. The audacity I have to challenge men armed with weapons! If there's one thing I know about gangsters and thugs, it is *not* to expect mercy. They only respond to a threat or intimidation that is higher than their own.

The young thug walks up close to me with the blade close to his face as if he's going to use it to give himself a shave. "It's foolish for you to run your mouth."

No, it's foolish to hold a knife close to your face in front of your enemy. I grab the thug's wrist and push the knife near his throat with a firm grip. The thug freezes in his steps and so do his counterparts. Never underestimate the element of surprise.

The other two thugs go into attack mode to try to gain advantage. Donny punches one in the sternum, and then drops him with an overhand right. Sammy distracts the other thug by letting him use himself as a punching bag. Donny comes to his father's aid by sneaking up behind the thug and putting him in a sleeper hold. I never take my eyes off the thug in front of me.

"Tell your boss, any message he has for me, he can bring to me directly." I know who he works for. Donny Moses looks at me, and I know he hears me.

"And I'll hold on to this." I hold up the knife.

"Mr. Demetrius will be in touch," the thug says as he moves away from the blade and walks back toward the Jeep he came in.

His two comrades pick themselves up off the ground and head toward the Jeep with him. I let out a deep sigh because I had no intention of killing a man; I just had to convince him that I was willing to do it. I went over to Donny to make sure he's okay.

"How are you?" I ask Donny.

"I'm fine," Sammy replies before his son could.

"I just had a knife pulled out on me," Donny says. "For six years, I've run my business and minded my own business and all of sudden, you show up, and now I'm getting weapons pulled out and my life is being threatened."

I feel like the lowest person on the planet. It's true, Donny has run a respectable business that has gone south ever I started using his charter services. More importantly, I will, one day, leave this island, but Donny will remain and this act of defiance can come back to haunt him.

"Listen, I'm sorry I got you mixed up in what I have going on, but I'll fix it. I promise you. I just need to get to the island and work everything out."

Donny starts shaking his head in disbelief. I'm sincere in what I'm saying, but I get the feeling that Donny doesn't believe me.

"Do you even *hear* yourself? I thought you were a man of God. A man of God doesn't run around getting mixed up with thugs and killers and whatever *else* you're mixed up in. You need to seriously rethink your calling, because I know that this . . ." He gestures with his hands and forms a circle . . . "This is not of God."

He's right, and there's no way I can justify my actions or say that I'm doing the will of God. I'm in pursuit of truth surrounding Pastor Cole's death, but do the ends justify the means? Given what has just transpired, I can't say it does.

"Listen, I know that I'm asking a lot, but I need you to fly me one more time to Green Cove. After that, we can sever all ties. I promise you."

Donny doesn't say anything for a long minute until he shakes his head and opens the door for us to get in. I'm grateful for Donny's compassion, but if this morning is any indication, then I'm in for a long day.

Chapter Twelve

We arrive at the hotel where the conference is taking place. Both Sammy and Victory know their roles. We have a snowball's chance in the lake of fire that my plan will actually work, but sometimes, we just have to roll the dice and see what we get.

"Now, are you sure that I ain't about to go to jail?" Sammy asks.

"I promise you that everything will be okay," I say.

Sammy cuts me with his eyes. He knows that there is a clear difference between the question he just asked me and the answer I just gave him. I look at Victory, and she adjusts her top, not wanting to reveal too much, but at the same time, wanting to be appealing to the eyes.

"You ready?" I ask her.

"Please, I once played Stella in the all-black version of *A Street Car Named Desire*."

"I bet you were phenomenal in it," I smile.

I feel bad about bringing Sammy and Victory into my coup, but I need certain distractions to pull off this next move. Victory walks over to the hotel reception desk. It takes only a millisecond for her to get the clerk's attention.

"Hello, ma'am, how can I assist you today?"

"Hi, I'm visiting Pastor Jackson, and I seem to have misplaced the key that he gave me. I was wondering if I could get a replacement key," Victory says smiling brightly.

"Sure, what's the room number?" the receptionist asks.

I'm within earshot and upon the question, Victory looks at me somewhat clueless as what to do next.

"Here is the thing, hon, I can't remember the room number. I don't pay attention to those kinds of details."

"Well, I'm sorry, ma'am, but I can't give you a new key without first verifying."

"What do you mean I can't get an upgrade of my room to a suite?" Sammy yells from the other side of the reception desk.

His voice was enough to cause a diversion, including the young man who is assisting Victory. While distracted, Victory reaches over the reception desk and touches the receptionist's hands.

"Listen, hon, you have bigger problems to worry about. Pastor Jackson won't mind. I *promise* you," Victory says seductively to him.

"I ain't going to lower my voice! Not until you upgrade my room free of charge!" Sammy says.

Stuck in a tight spot, the receptionist buries his head down in the computer screen. He types up a few things and hands Victory a key.

"Thanks, hon," Victory says with a sweet smile as she walks away.

Security has now arrived to escort Sammy off the premises. I meet Victory at the bottom of the staircase, and we both walk up side by side. I reach into my jacket and pull out a pair of latex gloves. No one can know I am here. Once I have the gloves on, Victory hands me the key.

When we arrive at Pastor Jackson's suite, I turn to Victory. "This is the part where we go our separate ways."

"Are you sure? I'm more than happy to help."

"That's okay. I can handle it. You just make sure that Sammy doesn't get hauled off to jail."

Victory gives me a warm smile, a head nod, and a kiss on the cheek as she touches my arm. "Be careful."

I watch her walk away, and I'm totally mesmerized. I know there will be a time where I will kick myself for not maximizing the opportunity I have with her, but now is not that time. I use the key to enter the room and once the door is closed, I start to go to work.

Pastor Jackson is unlike a lot of pastors I know. He's unapologetic. He doesn't apologize for his success, since he believes God has blessed him with it. He doesn't apologize for his remarks made during his sermons which often offend homosexuals and welfare recipients. He is convinced that everything he says is from the will of God and that's what makes him both a success and a target. The media can't get enough of Pastor Jackson and his latest bombastic statements. He acts as if he doesn't care. In that regard, maybe he and Pastor Cole have more in common than what I originally thought.

I search the room for evidence. Clearly, someone of his reputation has some skeletons hidden, but as I search through the drawers and closet, I can't find anything. I have to find something to leverage the information that I need from him.

Most people call what I'm doing blackmail, but that is such a strong word. I don't plan to use the information. I just need to *convince* Jackson that I *will* use it so that he can give me the information that I need.

I keep searching, but there's nothing here that I can use. Either Pastor Jackson is really careful, or he's more straitlaced than I thought. But why would he be here with the rest of the members of the elusive Cloth? I mean, granted, the Cloth is only known in relatively few circles, but these guys are not black ops agents. For a room to be as spotless as it is means that there is nothing to hide. I have keen insight, and I look in corners most people will overlook, which is why I considered a career in law enforcement years ago.

There is laughter in the distance, which means it's possible that Pastor Jackson is approaching. My original plan was to wait for him to return and strong-arm him into letting me know what Pastor Cole was up to before he was murdered. At this point, I have next to nothing to leverage. I only have the information I got on file from my friend, Paul. I don't know what to do. I thought about hiding in the closet. Maybe all Pastor Jackson would do is drop something off, and then leave, but that is not likely to happen. Things can go bad on so many different levels.

I decide the best position that shouldn't cause me to get a broken nose will be for me to have a seat in the chair next to the table. This gives me a less aggressive approach, which will not put Jackson on the defensive.

The voice gets closer and closer, and my heart forgets to beat for a moment or two. The door opens, and Pastor Jackson walks in. He is initially startled, but his eyes lock in on me, and he then starts grinning.

"What in the—You must be the guy I've heard about . . . Minister Dungy," Pastor Jackson says.

If Pastor Jackson can walk into a hotel room and know my name without ever meeting me, then that means one thing: someone talks too much, and that's not good.

"I guess my reputation precedes me," I say.

"That, among other things. You're not going to find anything. I keep this place so clean, CSI wouldn't be able to find anything."

I take my gloves off and stand up. I'm positive now that Jackson doesn't see me as a threat.

"So what do I owe this pleasure?" He walks over to the wet bar and fixes him a drink. He then looks toward me and motions to an empty cup.

I've been trying not to drink, not wanting to go back to that dark place in my life. This case, however, is far beyond me. I need something to take the edge off.

"Sure," I say as I walk toward the bar.

Pastor Jackson pours me a cup, hands it to me, and we toast. "To redemption."

"Redemption."

I take a hard swallow, and we both take a moment to recover from the force of a single malt.

"Let me guess . . ." Jackson takes a sip of his drink before he continues. "Paternity test?"

"Excuse me?"

"The running joke at my church is that once a week, a young girl comes forth claiming that I got her pregnant. Of course, the accusation is proven false. I like my women grown and on their own, but if you're here . . . then I wonder." Jackson takes another sip.

"I'm not here for any paternity suit."

"Then the only other reason why you would be here is to talk about Pastor Cole."

"How do you know?"

"Because I'm a prophet, Genius." Jackson laughs at his own sarcastic joke. "Why else would you be here?"

Pastor Jackson must have spies throughout the island keeping tabs on folks he deems as a threat. I'm sure I'm somewhere on that list.

"One of the benefits to being a prophet is that I'm intuitive, and the only way you would be here in my room is to ask me about Cole."

"I hear you guys were close."

"Elisha told you that?"

He is good, and I now know just how connected he is, and now comes the fun part. This means I would be able to uncover a lot of information from him. It also means I can take the gloves off.

"With all due respect, Pastor Jackson, I'm surprised to hear that you're a member of the Cloth."

Pastor Jackson erases his smile and sets his drink down on the table. "Now, Nic, I appreciate you trying to help out with Cole's investigation and all, but let it end there. You don't want to go too far off the path."

"You mean find out about you and all of your shady dealings?"

"You don't know anything, Nic, and that's your problem. You're a hypocrite, and what's worse is that you don't even *know* it."

"At least I'm not leading a whole congregation astray. I don't pretend to be something that I'm not."

Pastor Jackson gives me a dismissive wave. "All that self-righteous talk sounds nice, but let's be real with each other. You've made a living off of the shortcomings of your fellow brethren of the clergy. And you're going to judge *me* for being a part of an organization that seeks to help those same ministers?"

The difference is I try to get help for those ministers who I work with, and the Cloth offers them a place to indulge without judgment. It's sickening the duality that exists within this organization.

"So you, Cole, and Bryant would get together and counsel each other while in a room full of strippers and alcohol?" I ask.

"You sound worse than the women at my church. Look, the Cloth is not some religious mob. Any man who wants to leave can leave, so long as he maintains our code of silence."

That and a buyout to the tune of $50,000, I'm told. The Cloth keeps a tight noose around its members' necks. Maybe Cole found the noose too tight and wanted a way out. "So did Pastor Cole leave your organization?"

"That's none of your business. You're not a member of the Cloth, and I don't have to disclose that. And if I find out that Pastor Bryant has told you any of this, then he would be in violation of his confidentiality agreement."

"So Pastor Bryant is a part of the Cloth?"

I know the answer, but I like seeing the unflinching Pastor Jackson squirm, searching for an answer.

"Don't get cute with me, Nic. I know he asked you to look into Cole's death, but I know he didn't ask you to look into our organization. I'm going to say this, and I'm going to say this once, Nic. You don't want the Cloth as your enemy."

I could fill the Empire State Building full of nickels if I had one for every time someone threatens me. Pastor Jackson's threat may have teeth, but they're not sharp teeth.

"Listen, we can agree to disagree, but I'm trying to find out who would want to kill Cole," I say.

"Are you asking at Bryant's bidding or your owe curiosity?"

I'm starting to get annoyed by how much Pastor Jackson knows and why he is not inclined to share.

"Does it matter?"

My question causes Jackson to take another hard swallow of his drink. His eyes don't flinch as he looks at me.

"That's not going to happen," he says.

"I know you to be a man of faith, but how can you be so sure?"

"I just know," Jackson says.

"What was he involved in?"

"Not what, but *whom*," Pastor Jackson says with a smile.

"Randall Knott," I say.

"Randall Knott is just a businessman. Yeah, he and Cole had a falling out, but that was just business. Cole would have eventually come around and saw Knott's vision. I'm afraid my boy was caught up in some other stuff and messed around with a dark force."

Now I'm confused, and it's obvious that my facial expression conveys that confusion.

"My boy was dealing with Satan himself, in the form of a tantalizing woman," Pastor Jackson continues.

"Wait a minute. Hold on, are you telling me a woman might have killed Pastor Cole?"

"That's one way of putting it. Janae Hargrove. She is a local legend, a master of Obeah."

All Pastor Jackson had to say was the name Janae Hargrove. In the short time I've been on the island, I have become familiar with this woman by her reputation. She is a practitioner in black magic, and is otherwise known as a voodoo priestess.

Chapter Thirteen

I have graduated from stupid to crazy. That is the only way to describe the fact that I am on the boat at ten o'clock at night with Sammy Moses, heading to some voodoo queen's house. On any other night, this would be an exotic evening boat ride on warm Caribbean waters. Most advertisements for the Bahamas focus on the day and the beauty that exists on the island, but the night is a wonder to behold. This is an area of the world that isn't destroyed by smog, and where the moon and stars take center stage and reflect off the ocean. I wish that tonight I was on Sammy's boat with Victory, and we were on an aimless boat ride . . . but not this night.

The boat starts to slow down, and I begin to see a house that looks more like a hut in the corner of the island all by itself.

"There's the house you're looking for," Sammy says.

As the boat starts to slow down and the house starts to come into view, I start to second-guess my decision. The house looks like it shouldn't even be standing, let alone be a place of occupancy. There is no electrical power, at least none that I can see. There is only a glow from a fire, I presume from candles being lit which makes the house look like a jack-o'-lantern from a distance. Then the boat comes to a sudden stop.

"Is there something wrong?" I ask.

"No sir, there is nothing wrong," Sammy says.

"Well, then, why are we stopping?"

"We're stopped because this is as far as I will go. I can't go no farther," Sammy says.

I look at Sammy as if he has just cursed out my momma. I then look at the dock for the witch doctor's house, which is at least twenty feet away.

"You must have me mistaken for Carl Lewis, because there's no way I can jump from here," I point down at the boat, "to there," I point up to the dock.

"I reckon you're going to have to swim."

I know I am hearing what Sammy is saying. After all, he's saying it in plain English, but where I'm having a problem comprehending what Sammy is saying is the fact that he expects me to swim—fully clothed—to shore. The absurdity of the idea causes me to laugh.

"Look, Sammy, we talked about this back at Adele's house. You agreed to give me a ride to Janae's place, and we would go over there together. We agreed."

"You told me the plan, but I don't believe I actually agreed to anything. I agreed to give you a ride, but I didn't say anything about getting out of my boat."

"Sammy Moses! I *know* that's you out there!" a voice suddenly yells from the house.

I'm assuming that the woman yelling is Janae Hargrove. Now that she knows I'm here, I wonder how she knows Sammy Moses. I turn to Sam, and he is visibly shaken. He starts to power up his boat. At this rate, I may not even have a ride home.

"Sammy, how does she know you?"

Sammy puts his head down in shame, and I know that whatever he is about to tell me, this can't be good.

"Well, now, you see, Nic, when I first came out here to the island, I was alone and you know the Bible says that it's not good for a man to be alone. So . . . well . . . I met Janae, and that was before I knew about all this crazy stuff she's into and we-we . . ."

I give Sammy a dismissive wave; I don't need to hear anymore. Sammy's promiscuous transgressions have made an already nerve-racking situation worse. And so, with no real choice in the matter, I take off my sports coat, along with my shoes and socks, and dive into the water. I start swimming. The water is warm, and it feels good to cut through the ocean, even with wearing a cotton T-shirt and a pair of khakis. Since I'm used to swimming at least a mile a day, it takes me no time to arrive at shore. I look back at the boat, and even though it's dark, I see Sammy Moses waving me on like he's a coach whose been encouraging me this whole time. I look ahead to the house that is even more terrifying up close and begin to feel a little trepidation.

"God has not given me the spirit of fear or timidity, but of power and of love and of a sound mind." I conclude my prayer and start to walk inside the house. Out of the corner of my eye, I see Sammy's boat. I pray that it's still here when I come out.

Darkness can play with a man's mind. The door is open so I walk into Janae's house and that's all I see . . . *darkness* in a room only illuminated by a combination of red, black, green, and white candles. The candles are assembled in a triangle. I see wooden dolls positioned around the room as well. Some of the dolls are also candles. While I am somewhat spooked, I still trust in the power and authority I walk in with Jesus Christ. Lord knows I need Him right now.

Out of the darkness I see a white object being tossed toward me. It lands on the floor, and I see that it's a white towel.

"Don't track water on me floor, boy," a voice emanates out of the darkness.

I turn my head in search to where that voice originates. Out of the corner of the room is a woman with silver hair and a heart-shaped face sitting in a rocking chair. When she rocks forward, her face comes into view, and then fades into darkness. It's safe to presume that the woman in the chair is Janae. Now I'm starting to get even more spooked. *Lord, protect me from evil.*

"Well?" Janae motions to the towel.

I pick up the towel and start to dry off and wipe up the water on the floor.

"You have a lowlife for a friend," Janae says.

"I wouldn't say lowlife. Sammy doesn't always make sound decisions, but he's a good guy."

"You have a shaky definition of good, seeing that you had to swim here."

"I guess you're right about that. The Bible says there is no one who's righteous. I find there to be truth in that statement. I haven't met a single righteous man or woman in my lifetime. So we are all in need of grace, and we all are saved by grace as well.

"My name is Minister Dungy."

My name causes the woman to spring from her rocking chair and walk toward me. This woman couldn't be any more than four feet eleven inches tall, and yet, she has a very imposing aura about her.

"I'll tell you one thing like I told that other preacher. I ain't selling so you can leave my home if you know what's best for you."

The plot thickens. If Pastor Cole was the person that visited Janae, then he wasn't just out here for evangelism. Things still don't add up.

"I'm not here to buy. I mean, this is a lovely home and all, but that's not why I'm here."

Janae starts to laugh, and maybe it is a bit of an exaggeration on my part, but her laugh resembles that of a witch. "Then you're a bigger fool than I thought. You took a big risk, and for what?"

"Information."

Janae starts to laugh all over again. I realize that I may know more than she does, and I can use that to my advantage. Surprisingly, this island has gotten the better of me. It feels good to know something that the other person in the room doesn't know.

"I'm not buying, but I know who is, and I'm sure that Mr. Knott would make you a generous offer."

"Ain't enough money in the world he could offer me that would get me to sell. This is my family's legacy. We bled to make this ground fertile and beautiful and not for no man to come in with money and tell us to leave."

"Is that what you told my friend who came by with the same offer?" I ask.

"I told him I wasn't selling, and he went and told Mr. Knott. Now *you* are here."

Janae gives me a look of curiosity, and I am no longer intimidated by her aura. I see her as a woman clinging to her practice, hoping that it will be enough to scare people off.

"That preacher came up dead; do you know anything about it?"

The sudden shift in her posture is all I need to conclude a working theory I have: she doesn't know what happened to Pastor Cole. That's discouraging because here I am, standing in a witch doctor's house in wet clothes, and I'm still no closer to finding who killed Pastor Cole then I was before I jumped out of Sammy's boat.

"He couldn't have died. The cards didn't show death, only misfortune."

"The cards?" I immediately hate the fact that I ask that question.

Janae reaches to her right and pulls out a deck of cards. I know those are tarot cards, and I don't want any part of her practice. She starts to lay the cards out one by one.

"You know the practice of Obeah is illegal in the Bahamas?" I say.

"Just because it's legal don't make it right. Just because it's illegal don't make it wrong neither. Would you stop worshipping your God if it became illegal?"

Good point. Regardless of what my government mandates, I would still believe that Jesus died on the cross for my sins.

"So you still believe in your god, Satan?" I ask.

"Ignorant child, me don't believe in no devil. Me believe in nature and the ability to control and bend it."

"Well, you go ahead on believing that you can bend nature," I say.

If it's not for Christ, then it's for the ruler of this world which is Satan. But that's neither here nor there. I didn't come for a theological debate. I glance at the cards. Even in a poorly lit room, I can make out what each card represents. The first card is a picture of a fool. The next card is a picture of justice, but the final card is interesting. The final card is a picture of judgment.

"This is what you showed my friend?"

"The cards don't always reveal the future. Sometimes they reveal what's within," Janae says.

I believe that there isn't a force on this earth that can trump the power of God. If Pastor Cole was half the man that I think he was, he was powerful enough to pray off any hex or voodoo. Plus, I'm starting to doubt the legitimacy of Janae's craft.

"It would be wise to watch yourself. I see death in your future." Janae places the card of death on the table. "A whole lot of death."

"Yea though I walk through the valley of the shadow of death, I will fear no evil. You can keep your cards, my trust is in God."

Janae starts to laugh again; I guess she finds my scripture more amusing than reassuring. It doesn't matter; I know that those cards don't carry any more power than what I give them.

"Your friend said the same thing. Look what happened to him. God doesn't hear you. God exists in signs." Janae looks down at the cards.

She may see power written on those cards, but all I see is a bunch of spooky cards that should only be brought out during Halloween, if that.

"He hears me, and He'll see me through whatever comes my way."

Janae shrugs her shoulders. "I hope so, but tell your Mr. Knott that Janae Hargrove is not selling."

I turn to head toward the exit. I don't know why, but a picture from out of the corner of the room catches my eyes. It is a picture of a family of four. The picture is about the only normal thing in the entire room. Lord knows what happened to the father and the two boys with dreads. Lord only knows.

I walk out of Janae's house, and there is Sammy in the same spot. I don't want to go for a swim, but I really don't have much of a choice. One thing for sure. I don't plan on spending a night here with Janae.

Chapter Fourteen

"Nic!"

Hearing my name wakes me out of my sleep. Lord knows that last night was overwhelming, to say the least. Not to mention I have Randall Knott on one end and Demetrius on the other end. Pastor Cole is in between Knott and Demetrius, and I can't seem to figure out this puzzle.

"Nic, get your butt down here!" Adele yells from downstairs.

I can only imagine what I have done to warrant such a response. I hop out of bed and throw on a T-shirt and a pair of pants. A quick stretch after I slip on my shoes and I head down the steps before Adele calls again.

When I get downstairs, the front door is open and Adele is standing in the doorway blocking a large individual from entering. By the time I reach the bottom of the steps, I see that it's none other than Demetrius outside of the front door. Coincidence? I think not.

"This fool right here says he has an appointment with you." Adele doesn't take her eyes off Demetrius.

I don't think it matters if I have an appointment or not. Demetrius showed up at my door for a reason, and if I don't leave with him, things are going to get even more complicated.

"Yeah, I have an appointment."

"Hmm," is all Adele can say.

I start for the door but out of my peripheral I see Victory and the look is that of yet another day in which I am stepping out of the door. If this meeting with Demetrius goes south, then I feel even worse that this will be the last image I have of Victory. Her disappointment, her regrets, and there is no one to blame but myself.

"Let's go for a drive," Demetrius says.

That's the last thing a person would want a gangster to say to them because chances are . . . only one is going to return.

We drive to the marketplace on the island. Normally, I love coming here, but today, it seems solemn, like everything else. The marketplace has everything for trade or sell on the island from mangos to clothes to beads. Everything is available, and unlike back home, there's not a sense of competition, but rather a sense of community. Vendors are happy to recommend other places to go if they are out of stock.

There are no official parking spaces, so Demetrius pulls his black SUV in and parks on top of the hill. From the car, there is a dirt path we can walk down.

"Let's go and see what the market has to offer." Demetrius gets out of the car and closes the door.

After some hesitation I get out of the car as well. I walk alongside Demetrius, though I'm unsure why I'm here and what this is all about. Demetrius sees people and waves at them as if they are his longtime friends. He'll stop and talk with mothers and play with their children like a real pillar of his community.

"I've been to your California," Demetrius says.

How does he know I'm from California? Could there be a spy in my midst? Then again, through his associations, Demetrius has connections and can find out anything he wants.

"Oh yeah, how did you like it?" I ask.

"I didn't. The place is too crowded, no sense of community. Look at this," Demetrius pans around the crowd and businesses.

There is laughter and conversations going on. I understand why someone from the islands would come to the States and be put off by the cutthroat world of commerce. We walk through the crowd that has already gathered and stopped by a fruit stand.

"Good morning, Katherine, how are you?" Demetrius asks.

Katherine doesn't respond to Demetrius; she doesn't even smile. She just stops preparing her display of various passion fruits, turns around, and goes into the back of her stand. Demetrius does not take his eyes off of her as she bends down.

"She has a nice boom-boom, doesn't she?" Demetrius elbows me with a perverted smile on his face.

Moments later she returns with a vanilla envelope.

"Much appreciated," Demetrius says. He smiles as he takes the envelope and a piece of fruit and walks away.

I know for a fact that it doesn't take much capital to start a fruit stand. So the payment Katherine just made to Demetrius is more for the pleasure to operate in his territory. We walk down a few more stands to a jewelry stand. Everything is handmade and beautiful. I think Victory likes this kind of jewelry. It will help to smooth over the fact that once again, I'm not around to spend time with her.

"Hello, Laura. How are you?" Demetrius says to the jewelry shop owner.

Laura doesn't even bother to use English, but it's safe to assume that she and I have the same sentiments toward Demetrius. My Creole is a bit rusty, but I can recognize some of the words she uses. Laura goes to the corner of

her stand and produces an envelope. She doesn't hand it to
Demetrius; she *throws* it at him and gives him some more
hot Creole to go along with it.

"Always a lady, Laura," Demetrius says.

I look down at her stand and see a crucifix necklace
made out of beads. No fancy jewels went into this design,
but anyone who knows anything about jewelry would
marvel at the skill in making this necklace. I hold up the
necklace for Laura to see.

"How much for the necklace?" I ask.

"Five," she says.

I reach into my pocket to pull out my wallet. The dollar
is widely accepted in the Bahamas.

"Don't worry about that, friend, it's on the house,"
Demetrius states.

Laura looks like she wants to scratch his eyes out as
he hands me the necklace. Demetrius starts walking,
and when he's not looking, I drop a twenty-dollar bill on
Laura's table to pay for the necklace and the trouble.

Demetrius makes several similar stops along the way.
Some of the people he collects from didn't even bother
to put the money in an envelope. They just hand it to
Demetrius, and he keeps moving along to the next vendor.
The last stop is also a fruit stand, but the owner gives
Demetrius not only an envelope, but a fruit basket. Deme-
trius slips two of the envelopes he collected into the bottom
of the basket and keeps walking.

At the end of the market is a patrol car with two
local police officers standing by it, resting on their heels.
Demetrius does not break stride as he approaches them
and hands them the basket. All out in the open and now it
becomes clear why Demetrius wants me here . . . to instill
the point that no money is earned or spent without his
approval.

The two cops size me up. They are taking mental notes of me. They don't like me, and the feeling is mutual. I hate crooked cops. I know hate is a strong word and a word that contradicts the Christian doctrine, but I don't know what other word to use.

"This is my friend Nicodemus Dungy. I'm showing him around." Demetrius gives me a pat on the back like we are longtime friends.

That is also Demetrius letting me know that he found out my name along with everything else he could know about me from another source.

"Let's go, friend, I have so much to show you." Demetrius gives me a second pat on the back as he starts to head back toward the marketplace.

I know one thing for sure: if I come up missing, I can guarantee that these two gentlemen of the law will *not* go looking for me.

We walk back through the marketplace. It takes us less time to get back to the car since we didn't have to make any stops. I climb back in just as perplexed as I was when I first left the car.

"What's this all about?" I ask.

"I've got a business proposition for you, but first, I would like for you to see how I do business."

"Shaking down honest businesspeople . . . I think I have a clear idea of how you do business," I say.

"You are one biggety fellow, Mr. Dungy."

Biggety means bold, which, at times, I have been really bold. But I'm not bold enough to shake down a marketplace and bribe two police officers in broad daylight. I'm not even bold enough to *not* get in the car with Demetrius.

"Say what you will, but I don't like the way you do business," I tell him.

"Come then, let's see if you will like the way I do business after my next stop."

Demetrius turns on the engine and starts to drive. We drive down the road. I don't think it has even been ten minutes before he pulls into a parking space along the side of the island. This is the part of the island where the residents are more likely to have a boat instead of a car.

It's an area reserved for people who love waking up to the smell of saltwater and are not threatened by the hurricane season. The location is near the rocks, and a person can push their boat off into the ocean and float along the way. That whole process would take no more than five minutes at the most.

Demetrius gets out of the car, and I follow him up a walkway toward a house that sits on top of the hill. Walking up the hill I wonder if this was going to be the place where Demetrius kills me. I have no bargaining chip that would ensure my survival. I can't even guarantee the safety of Victory.

Which leaves me to wonder if I am better off trying to survive this attack than just being the noble knight who falls on his sword. Chivalry is about as dead as I will be if I don't think of a better plan.

Demetrius knocks on the door so hard it can be heard at the bottom of the hill. Moments later, the door opens, and it's a little boy.

"Hi, Uncle Demetrius," the boy says, not with joy, but with terror.

"Is your father home?" Demetrius asks.

The boy nods his head and opens the door to reveal two of his siblings. Both are boys and there's not much of an age difference between them. I'm confused and terrified for what's about to unfold.

"Who's at the door?" a man says from upstairs.

"Uncle Demetrius," the boy says.

Footsteps soon follow, and a man emerges from the top of the staircase. His steps down slow as the sight

of Demetrius and I come into view. Demetrius's grin is
borderline demonic.

"Hello, friend," Demetrius says.

It's safe to say that the gentleman before me is not
Demetrius's brother, but his business dealings are frequent
enough where the kids have come to view him as a relative.

"Hello, Demetrius."

"David, this is my good friend, Nic. I'm showing him
around the island."

David doesn't take his eyes off Demetrius. Judging
from his eyes, fear starts to take more of a stronghold
with each word Demetrius says to him.

"I'm sorry. I was going to bring it to you."

Demetrius waves off the man's explanation, and instead,
he reaches into his back pocket and pulls out his Beretta
and smacks David with the butt of the gun.

David falls flat on his wallet and tries to scoot away
from Demetrius. He reaches into his front pocket and
holds the money up toward Demetrius.

"The fact that I have to come here is disrespect enough."
Demetrius reaches down and snatches the money.

Demetrius is about to reach back and smack the guy
again when I intervene by stepping in between him and
David. I put my hands up to prevent Demetrius from
advancing.

"Come on, man, not in front of the children," I say.

Demetrius looks at me before he tosses me off to the
side with such velocity that I fall to the floor.

"Don't ever touch me." Demetrius takes a look at the
young boys who are terrified at the scene that has just
unfolded. "Not to worry. I'm not going to kill him because
then, who would look after my nephews?"

The boys seem too terrified to respond. Demetrius just
puts the money in his pocket and walks out the door. I
gather myself up off the floor and help David off the floor
as well.

"I'm sorry about that," I say to David.

I don't know why I have a habit of apologizing for another person's actions, but I do. I look at the boys, and they are in tears. I look back at David, and he is on the verge of tears. Young boys who are fortunate to have their fathers in their lives often look up to their fathers as titans. It's heartbreaking to see a titan toppled like these boys have just seen.

"I'm sorry," I say to the boys before I walk out the door.

Once outside, I see Demetrius is at his truck having a cigar. He's not even the least bit disturbed by his actions. I guess that's how monsters operate.

"Hey, I'm not about to ride around with you and watch you terrorize people," I say.

"I needed to make a few stops before I show you what I want you to see."

Demetrius tosses his cigar on the ground and stumps on it with his foot before he gets into the truck. It would be too much to walk back to Adele's from here, so I head to Demetrius's truck and climb inside.

From the house we drive along the one main road on the island. There are two peaks on the island and on the far right peak, Demetrius's house sits, but on the opposite end of the island there is flat land with a breathtaking view of the island. Demetrius parks the car, and I get out. He walks to an edge with his hands in his pocket, looking out into the ocean like a man on top of the world. I stand next to him with my hands also in my pockets taking in the view.

"My grandfather was a great businessman. He ran a landscaping business in Miami and a fishing business out here. He bought up land real cheap. When he died, he owned a fair portion of the island. My father built upon what my grandfather did and expanded. My father bought more land, including a nice hidden spot on the island that made it look like our own little paradise. I followed in his footsteps. I built houses on land we owned, and I rent them out to folks. I expanded our business in the world of imports and exports."

Demetrius smiles at his accomplishments. "You know, there wasn't even an airport at Crystal Cove until about fifteen years ago. For that whole time, I would have planes land and take off. No one would bother me. That was, until Randall Knott showed up."

I wonder how this inspiring story of a man who starts from nothing and accomplishes everything gets twisted and turns into a drug kingpin. It goes back to man's unquenched thirst for more. Demetrius taps me on the shoulder to follow him. We walk back to the truck and Demetrius pulls out a map and spreads it across the hood of his truck. He uses both hands to hold the map down to keep it from flying away due to the wind.

"Randall Knott is trying to take land that I own. He's trying to steal from me, and your buddy was sent here to do his bidding."

"That doesn't make sense. Why would Pastor Cole do anything on Knott's behalf?" I ask.

"Are you calling me a liar?" Demetrius questions.

I didn't respond to him, but I did notice the spot Demetrius had circled. "You think this is the land that Knott wants to purchase?"

"That is the land he's trying to steal."

I walk away from Demetrius back to the edge. This time, instead of looking out at the ocean, I look down at the bottom of the cliff and see a shack. A shack that I'm very familiar with. It is a shack owned by Janae the witch doctor.

"My father built her that house so that she could have a slice of heaven," Demetrius says.

I think he knows that I now have connected the dots and that this land Demetrius is fighting for, and possibly killing for, is the land where his mother lives. I turn back around and walk toward him.

"So why not fight it out in court?" I ask.

"If we involve the courts, then they start prying into all of my affairs. I can't allow that to happen."

Demetrius is in quite a conundrum. Someone is committing a crime against him, but Demetrius has committed crimes himself. He can't afford for his misdeeds to come to light.

"So what do you need me to do?"

"I don't need you to do anything. I want you to find out what Knott is planning to build on that land. Now Adele and that pretty gal of yours, they need you."

"I don't care who you are. You can't threaten me, and you won't harm either one of them."

Demetrius laughs while I ball my fists up ready to strike. I'm sick and tired of his threats, and I refuse to tolerate them any longer.

"Then we have an understanding. You find out what I need to know, and I stay away from your loved ones."

Demetrius gives me a pat on the back and walks back to the car. I get in because in my heart of hearts, I know that the only way I can protect Adele, Sammy, and Victory is if I find out what Knott is up to and try to stop him.

On the way back there wasn't much of a conversation between the two of us. We just rode along a bumpy road until something pierces the window. I figure it was a shot, and from a distance there was an image of a person I couldn't make out standing on the road.

"What the . . ." I say.

Demetrius bends down and pulls a gun from under his seat. Another shot pierces the window and hits Demetrius in the arm. He loses control of the truck and starts to swerve. The truck flies off the road, and all I see is a lagoon that the SUV is headed toward.

Chapter Fifteen

This warm water I've come to love may be what takes me down. The water is rising, and we are sinking. I'm barely conscious, and Demetrius is unconscious. The water is above my shoulders, and I have to move and the passenger window is open, but I can't leave Demetrius. Right now, he's 300 pounds of dead weight.

"Lord Jesus, please help me, Lord."

I start to kick the windshield. Once it's out, the water will come rushing in, but that's the only chance I have to get Demetrius out of the car, and at this point, it could be for nothing. For all I know, he could be dead.

When the windshield is kicked out and the water is rushing in, I grab ahold of Demetrius and struggle to pull him out of the car. I've got to calm down and slow my heart rate. I can't panic—don't panic! I need to get air soon, but I have to get Demetrius out. I pull him out. I'm pulling and pulling, and I'm not making much progress. This can't be how this ends. Lord, please help me!

I reach around and secure Demetrius by his belt. Don't panic, Nic, you're going to make it. I push as hard as I can with my legs and finally we start to ascend. We break through the water, and I get one gulp of air until I sink back down.

I don't think I have anymore to give, but if God gives me the strength to get above water once, He'll do it twice. I push as hard as I can, and we get above water again. I get another gulp of air and start swimming to shore. With every stroke of my free hand, I feel like I'm either going to sink or lose Demetrius.

I close my eyes because I don't want to lose hope. I don't want to think about how far I have to swim with Demetrius or how tired I am or how I might not survive this whole ordeal. I finally touch land and with the last bit of all my strength, I pull myself and Demetrius onto shore.

I roll over on my back, still trying to catch air and steady my breathing. My arms are on fire and my legs are burning from exhaustion, but I am elated. It takes so much for me to turn over and observed Demetrius, who is lifeless.

I start trying to do CPR, and when that doesn't work, and though I hesitate for a moment, I even start to do mouth-to-mouth. It took a long moment, but Demetrius suddenly spits up water and starts to cough. Thank you, Jesus! Demetrius is alive. I am alive. Thank you, Jesus. Now, the question is . . . Who shot at us?

God has a way of humbling some and mystifying others. Here I am in an unknown part of the island with a man who has threatened me on more than one occasion and has threatened those who I care about. Yet, I save *his* life, while my life is *still* in danger. And now there's an assassin on the loose. I sit with the mosquitos biting my skin and the sun blazing down. Demetrius sits beside me, lost and confused. Lord have mercy.

"We need to keep moving," I say right after I finish tying a piece of my shirt around Demetrius's arm to stop the bleeding. We need to leave, but I barely have the strength to go on, let alone carry an enormous man like Demetrius around.

"Yeah, we should," Demetrius says before he gets up and starts to walk.

"You know where you're going?" I ask.

"I know every inch of this island. My uncle used to take me fishing in that very same lagoon. I didn't think I would almost die in it."

Neither did I. We walk through the jungle, and it hasn't escaped my attention that the truck ending up in the lagoon is not the result of careless driving but rather someone trying to kill us.

"Who do you think did this?" I ask.

"I don't know," Demetrius says.

"Guess," I say.

"There can be only one man stupid enough to do this. Stupid enough to think he's protected."

I know who Demetrius thinks it is, but just because all roads point to Randall Knott doesn't mean that Randall Knott is the shooter. The world operates in a gray area more often than black and white.

"I saw someone on the road. I couldn't make them out, but they had to be following us," I say.

"There was no one following us," Demetrius says.

"How can you be so sure?"

"Because no one is stupid enough to follow me. It's suicide."

Apparently we have one stupid assassin running about, and Demetrius doesn't have a clue as to the assassin's true identity.

"You know, pride goes before a fall," I say.

"What's that supposed to mean?"

"Don't let your ego be your downfall. I still think the assassin is out there."

"No, there was no assassin out there looking for us." Demetrius checks his arm.

"No? You sound so sure."

"Had he been a professional, he would've fired a few more shots into the car and made sure that we didn't surface to the lagoon."

"Maybe he was in a rush."

"There's no one around for miles and miles. He had time. No, he thought that a few shots and the truck going into the water was enough. He was sadly mistaken."

"By the grace of God we survived this crash," I say.

"God doesn't have nothing to do with it. We got lucky."

The man survives being shot and his truck going over a cliff and yet he doesn't believe he has been spared for a reason. I know who spared me, and I know who gave me the strength to drag a man twice my size to the shore.

"We need to get going. It'll be dark soon," Demetrius says.

"Lead the way."

We walk for hours, but the jungle is so thick and massive that we hardly put a dent into it. The sun fades into distant memory and soon the night approaches. I continued to follow Demetrius as he leads through the jungle, stepping through plants, fighting off bugs and God knows what.

"It's getting dark. We'll need to stop for the night," Demetrius says.

"We got to keep going." I can barely talk.

"We will not make it back tonight. We have to rest and start again at first light. We'll make it back by tomorrow."

Tomorrow seems so far away and such a long shot. Demetrius needs medical attention, and I'm about to pass out from exhaustion.

"We'll be okay for tonight," Demetrius says.

That's *if* we can survive this night. Right now, it doesn't look good.

Chapter Sixteen

Darkness is not kept at bay on the island. It's allowed to reign through the night unchallenged by anything except for the moon. I sat next to a tree, unable to see what's in front of me. I'm starving and borderline dehydrated. I feel like there are bugs crawling all over me and my ears are playing tricks on me because I'm hearing all kinds of disturbing things go bump in the night.

A song starts to resonate within. I'm not much of a singer, but at this moment I feel compelled to sing. I also feel that part of me that would sound silly. Demetrius is close by, at least I think he's close by. I can't hear him snore, so I wonder what Demetrius is thinking. He almost died today, and now with an assassin running about, thoughts of mortality have to be weighing heavily. For me, I am grateful to be alive, and I sing a song of praise.

"There is none like you. No one else touches my heart like you do, and I can search for eternity, Lord, and find, there is no one like you."

I must admit that of all the hymns and Christian songs, this does not rank as one of my personal favorites, but in the dark in a jungle, with a drug dealer beside me and a murderer on the loose, I feel compelled to express that there is no one like God who has kept me this whole time, and I consider myself grateful if I make it to see another day.

"Why do you to pray to a God that doesn't exist?" Demetrius broke my cadence.

He must've not been impressed with my musical talents.

"How do you know that He doesn't exist?"

"Do you know how many men have begged and prayed to God right before I killed them, and God did not answer?"

Demetrius now is completely comfortable to show me his dark passenger. He mustn't think that we are going to survive this catastrophe; otherwise, he would remain silent.

"So, because God didn't answer, that means He doesn't exist?"

"I thought the whole point was to answer prayer."

"The point is redemption, faith, hope, and trust. God does not answer every prayer, but the purpose of faith is trust that Jesus is your salvation and trust in God's plan even when you come to the end of your life."

Demetrius laughs, and given our current set of circumstances, his laugh is between cynical and demonic.

"You laugh, but it's my faith that caused me to pull you out of a sinking truck when most people would have let you drown."

"You saved me because you're afraid of what my men would do if they thought you were responsible for killing me."

"I think your men would give me a fist bump if I did. Fear and love can't coexist. You rule through fear, but the Bible shows that people will do more out of love than fear."

"I take care of their families."

"How many families do you destroy in the process?" My question went unanswered.

"Thank you," Demetrius says.

I don't need to ask what he is thanking me for because I already know. He's thanking me for saving his life.

God is a great teacher, because in most people's book, Demetrius deserves to die, but God believes that all men and women deserve a chance at redemption.

"Don't mention it," I say.

"If you want to go to sleep, I can take first watch. You can sleep," Demetrius says.

"No, I'm good. I'll stay up first," I say.

"Have you way then."

I hear movements, and though I can't make anything out. I figure it's Demetrius positioning himself to try to get some sleep. I close my eyes with the tune still stuck in my head.

"I can search for all eternity, Lord, and find there is no one like you. No one else can do my heart like you do."

This time the song didn't come from me, but from Demetrius. I get the sense that his parents did take him to church at one point, and while his beliefs may remain unchanged, at least for the moment he finds comfort in this song. All I can do is join in.

God gave Demetrius and me a beautiful gift. He allowed us to see another sunrise, and I know that the fact that this sunrise was not promised is what makes me welcome the warmth of the sun.

"Thank you, Jesus."

Demetrius didn't say anything. He just stands up with his eyes closed and embraced a sun that we have experienced a million times, but on this day, the sun felt new.

"I don't know how I would've made it without you," Demetrius says.

"I don't know how I would've made it without Him." I point upward.

Demetrius didn't make a sly remark. He just glanced at the sun one more time, and then he looked forward. "This is the way home."

It took several more hours of no food and water. The sun that embraced us earlier now beat on us. I keep wondering when the moment will arrive when I can't walk anymore and I will finally collapsed, but that moment did not come.

"You go ahead," Demetrius says, leaning against a tree. "Go and get help. The main road is just over that hill."

"Are you kidding me? I didn't drag you out of a lagoon to leave you."

Again, the easier thing to do would be to leave Demetrius and head on home. But the scriptures say in Matthew that whatever permits you to go one mile with a man, go with them two. With that bit of instruction, I walk over to Demetrius and place his arm around my shoulder. We start to walk, and my legs buckle from his weight.

"Come on, Demetrius, I need you to walk with me. We're almost there."

We walk; we stumble and fall; but we eventually arrive at the top of hill where I can see the back of Adele's house at the bottom of the hill. I fall to my knees. "Thank you, Jesus."

"Don't thank Him just yet. We still have a hill to climb."

I find the strength to climb down the hill and Demetrius follows me. He too finds renewed strength at almost being home. We walk down the hill, and my legs feel like they'll give out on me at any minute.

When we get to the bottom of the hill, Demetrius and I just stand there on the main road trying to catch our breath. I also believe that he and I were in disbelief that we survived.

"I'm sorry for threatening you and your family," Demetrius says in between long breaths.

What could I say to that? At this point I have to question Demetrius's sincerity and pay close attention to his actions.

"I'm going to meet with Randall Knott and find out what he's up to with the other preachers."

"Better hurry. The conference is over in two days," he says.

Then that means I have two days to wrap this up. I gather my last ounce of strength and walk toward Adele's house. My home in Carson is thousands of miles away, but Adele's place feels like home as I knock on the door.

"Where have you been?" Adele asks.

"It's a long story that I don't have time to tell."

It takes her a moment, but she starts to smell me and backs away as she covers her nose.

"I'll tell you once I have a shower. Where's Victory?" I look around, but I don't see her in sight.

Adele has a sad look in her eyes as if there is something she does not want to tell me. She doesn't have to tell me because I already know. Victory is gone. She left because I broke the only real rule she had: Don't promise too much. Promise only what you can deliver.

Chapter Seventeen

I'm convinced that Randall Knott has had a hand in Pastor Cole's death. My time in the jungle with Demetrius tells me that he wouldn't go as far as to kill an innocent man. He only kills those in the criminal world who cross him. All of his threats are hollow, and most of the locals are fooled. The real threat is Knott, and now I have to get to him, but I can't focus on Randall Knott until I first deal with the fact that Victory is gone. I shouldn't be surprised, and Lord knows that a good woman would've left days ago. Victory is a rare and special woman with the gift of patience, but I now know that her patience has a limit. Whatever I hope to accomplish and all aspirations of a relationship have faded away. I now sit at the edge of my bed with a letter Victory wrote, too afraid to read it.

"Nic," Adele says as she enters the room.

"Hey, Adele, I'm sorry if you were worried about my whereabouts."

"Not as worried as Victory was. You darn near gave that girl a heart attack. Where were you?"

"I had to see Demetrius again," I say.

"You're not mixed up in the foolishness that he's mixed up in?"

"No, nothing like that. I just had to see him."

That pricks my heart to hear that Victory was worried about that until she finally decided that it's better for her to leave then to wait for me to come home with a new excuse.

"There is something wrong with a man who can't find rest, even when he's on vacation. I think Victory understood that," Adele says before she looks at my letter. "Read the letter. Lord willing, it will help set your mind at ease."

I just look at the letter, still not motivated to actually read it. I imagine that I will feel worse after I have read it.

"Dinner will be ready soon," Adele says as she leaves.

I sit there on my bed and finally open the letter.

> *Dear Nic,*
>
> *I'm sorry that my departure from the island is abrupt, but I believe that it is necessary. I came to the island because I wanted to know what it would be like if you and I were to give us a shot. I now have my answer, and though I think you're a great guy, I don't think a relationship is the kind of thing you need right. I wish you all of the best and pray that you will blessed.*
>
> *God bless,*
> *Victory*

I close the letter and think how on any other day I would agree with her, but not today. Today, I feel like I can be the man that Victory needs, and that I can have a life outside of the problem-solving business. But Victory is gone . . . but how far could she have gone?

I run downstairs into the kitchen where Adele and Sammy are having a conversation, and it appears that they are actually enjoying their conversation for once.

"What's up, Doc?" Sammy asks.

"How long ago did Victory leave?"

"About this morning before you came back," Adele replies.

"She hitched a ride with my son back to Miami."

Miami is a two-hour flight; it's possible that I can get to her in time. Forget about Pastor Cole and who murdered him. I'll give Pastor Bryant back his money, but Victory is a once-in-a-lifetime woman, and I'm not going to let her go. I have to find a way to make things right with her.

"I need—" before I could even finish, Sammy tosses me the keys to his truck.

"You better hurry up, Romeo."

I run out the door not sure of what I would say if I did catch up to Victory.

I arrive at the airport, and my heart sinks when I see several police cars surrounding Donny Moses' plane. I see German shepherds go into his plane while Donny stands off to the side with his hands cuffed.

Two police officers emerge from Donny's plane with two bags that have been duct taped. Drugs—yes, but were they Donny's—no. Duct tape and plastic wrap, which makes it hard for the dogs to sniff. This is the circus, and the show has been planned from the beginning. Someone has planted the drugs on Donny's plane, and the whole ordeal is not even to get to Donny but to get to me.

I get on the phone and call Sammy to tell him that his son is being hauled off to jail, but another call comes through from a number that I don't recognize.

"Hello?" I say.

"Minister Nicodemus Dungy, this is Randall Knott. I would like to speak with you regarding an urgent matter."

The devil has revealed himself and wants to have a conversation. This is one meeting that I can't afford to miss.

Chapter Eighteen

In light of what has transpired today, I'm force to take a long hard look at how I ended up in this situation. Victory is gone, and Donny is in jail. I stand on the same tarmac where hours ago I watched an innocent man get carried off. Now I await a private plane to land and pick me up. I am off to see the wizard.

I see from a distance a Gulfstream jet descending onto the runway. That's my ride. I wonder if Knott is on the plane or is this one expensive taxi ride. The plane lands and pulls to a stop. The door opens, and a man of Haitian descent disembarks.

"Mr. Dungy. Right this way," he says.

I hate this fake act of chivalry, but I have to endure this charade until I can get back and get Donny out. I walk on board the plane and sure enough, Knott is not on it. He wants me to come to him.

I realize that my biggest error has been my approach to this whole situation. I have approached this situation as Nicodemus Dungy on vacation. I need to approach this situation as Nicodemus Dungy, the guy who's not afraid to get his hands dirty.

The plane lands on the ground, and this time, there is a Mercedes truck waiting to take me to Randall Knott's home. Cameron was also to the far right trying to wave me down.

"Tell Mr. Knott I will meet up with him."

"My orders are to bring you straight to Mr. Knott's residence."

I am a freeman, and I won't let any man push me around or tell me what to do. I don't care. "Don't worry; I didn't hop on the plane to be a no-show. I just have to make a stop somewhere first, but I won't keep Mr. Knott waiting."

I don't even wait for an answer, I just walk past the truck and toward Cameron. For once I'm glad to see him.

"What up, fam? Where can Cameron take you this fine day?"

"I need to buy a new suit, and I need to meet up with someone."

"Not to worry, fam, Cameron got you."

I couldn't meet Randall Knott dressed like a member from Gilligan's Island. I needed to get myself cleaned up for this meeting.

I am not a fan of buying off the rack. I don't consider myself pretentious, I just have an appreciation for the feel of a tailor-made suit. At the suit shop on the island, I wasn't able to find my traditional smoking gray suit, so I choose a black-on-black suit and shades. I felt like a new man cruising along the town as Cameron recklessly weaves in and out of traffic.

"You sure you know where you're going?" I ask.

"Cameron knows where Mr. Knott lives; everybody knows, fam," Cameron says over his shoulder.

Cameron guns his bike and starts to make his way up a steep hill. The higher Cameron climbs, the more an estate starts to come into view. I now know why Cameron didn't need an address. The house is more like a Mediterranean palace with high Greek pillars. It's clear from the house that only one man could live there, and that man is Randall Knott.

"That's Mr. Knott's house. One day, Cameron is going to live there. Just you wait and see."

Faith is a very powerful tool. It runs counter to logic and reason. Those two entities are grounded in what is and what can be ascertained. Faith is ground in the possibilities of what could be. It takes faith for someone like Cameron, who is currently operating a taxi service, to believe that he can one day aspire to live on the top of the mountain.

It takes several minutes before we arrive at the top of the hill. Knott's home is Greek inspired with two pillars standing in the entranceway. I'm surprised that there wasn't a security gate put in place for Knott's protection.

Moments later, several men emerged from the front door with weapons drawn. That explains the reason why he doesn't need a security gate. He wants to enjoy his view of the island without it being obstructed by metal bars. He would rather hire a small mercenary team to greet any unwanted guest.

"Don't worry, fam, Cameron got you." Cameron flashes his .22 pistol.

We would have a better chance with a paintball.

"That's okay, Cameron, I got this." I caution for Cameron to put his gun away to avoid escalating the situation.

The presence of the security is to prove a point to me; I can't even get the notion of trying any funny business or that would be all she wrote.

"Boys, come on now, don't scare away my guest," Randall Knott says.

The security guards break away, and Randall Knott emerges with a cigar in his mouth. He's much taller than I thought. Knott is in his late sixties, but he has a full head of hair, and it's all silver.

"I'm sorry about that, Minister Dungy. My boys get bored easily, so they'll jump at the first thing that moves."

"Not a problem. I understand."

"I tell you this much, it's a lot easier to be a billionaire when you have former SEALs and black ops watching your back."

If Randall Knott is trying to intimidate me with his money and influence, then I will say that this is an epic failure. In the last week, I have met with a witch doctor, been threatened, shot at, and dumped by my pseudo-girl-friend. I'm neither intimidated nor scared.

"Let's go inside and cool down." Knott pats me on the back.

I follow him into his home and was blown away by the décor. I'm not easily impressed. I despise opulence, but this house was designed for a Pharaoh.

Now the outside of the home may be influenced by early Greek architecture, but the inside of the home is pure Bohemian influence. With an impressive collection of seashells and ceiling fans, the home remained quite cool. I wonder how many times Knott visits this island during the course of the year. I'm sure he comes down whenever he's tired of the cold weather.

"I know you're a religious man, but can I offer you a drink?"

I see two glasses at the bar, one that Knott is pouring a single-malt scotch into, and the other glass is empty.

"Sure," I say. I need to establish that I'm not a strait-laced preacher so that Knott will be comfortable to tell me what's going on. That shouldn't be too hard.

"This single malt would be the death of me . . . if my four ex-wives don't kill me first," Knott says before he lets out a big laugh.

Only an egocentric nonbeliever would find being divorced multiple times amusing.

"So help me fill in the blanks." Knott hands me my drink. "You go to college at San Francisco State and get a degree in sociology. You attend seminary and work in ministry for a local church, and then you drop off the face of the earth until about five years ago."

Someone has done their homework. So have I. "So what's your question?"

"I guess the question is, what do you do, Minister Dungy?"

A person doesn't fly a G-5 jet to pick up someone just to find out what they do for a living. Randall Knott knows; he just wants me to tell him.

"I specialize in fixing church problems, in particular, problems that the church may be having with its leaders."

My job description really piqued Knott's interest. "So, you're in the public relations business?"

"More like private relations. I handle matters that churches and certain organizations would not want to see become public."

"Interesting. That's very interesting. I need someone like you on my payroll."

That's all Knott said before he returns back to the bar to fix himself another drink. I'm still working on my first drink and a way to uncover why Randall Knott is using the church convention to acquire property.

"So why are you not with the rest of them at the conference?"

"Because even though they need me, that don't mean that they like me." Knott flashes a smile similar to the one that he flashed on the cover of *Forbes*.

"I know about that all too well. I have my detractors all over, including right here in the Bahamas," Knott says.

"You mean Demetrius?" I'm not one to beat around the bush.

Knott takes a sip of his drink, and then points his glass at me as if I just guessed the correct answer.

"Exactly. He's a strange guy to figure out. I offer him a fortune to acquire some land, and he turned it down."

"Some people care more about their family's legacy than money. Maybe you haven't studied your opponent enough."

"Oh, that's a load. When someone tells me that they're not selling because of their family legacy, to me, that translates to I want more money."

I guess one of the requisites for being a self-appointed master of the universe is the mentality that money solves everything. Knott has this idea that there isn't anything of value that he couldn't put a dollar sign to and purchase.

"You may be right, but I don't believe I'm here to settle Bahamian property disputes because I'm not qualified to do so."

Knott starts to laugh, and then he finishes his drink.

"Listen, I'm having a get-together at my hotel on the island where you currently stay. I would love for you to attend. I'll send a boat to pick you up around eight o'clock."

That was exactly what I need, a peek behind the current.

"I would love to be there, but there is just one small matter to discuss and forgive me for assuming, but I have a pilot friend who was arrested for something he didn't commit."

Knott is not at all surprised by my declaration. There is no doubt in my mind that Knott is the one that made the call.

"Well, that's unfortunate. I'll tell you what. I'll make some calls and see what I can do."

He didn't admit to being the one who set Donny Moses up; of course, he wouldn't, but as I left Mr. Knott's home, I'm sure that this matter will be resolved by the time I get back to the island.

Chapter Nineteen

I arrive at the police station expecting that the process of getting Donny Moses released would be seamless since it was Knott who put him there in the first place. Imagine my surprise when I arrive at the front desk and see that no one is here. A bell sits in front of me, so I start to ring it, and I keep ringing it until a police officer comes running out of the back room and snatches the bell from me.

"What you banging on me bell like that for?"

"I'm sorry. It's just that no one was here," I say.

"Of course someone is here. What do you think? We leave the prisoners here by themselves?"

"I didn't mean it like that."

"Who done hammered up all my bread, man?" The officer holds up a plate with only the crumbs on it. He then turns around before he sets his sights back on me. "Was it you?"

"No," I say while being thrown off by his question.

He stares at me for a long minute. "What do you want?"

"I'm here to pick up Donny Moses. He's supposed to be released."

The man starts rummaging through papers looking for something I don't know what.

"Daniel," he calls out to the back.

There is some rumbling in the background and soon a man twice the size of the officer appears with his shirt not tucked in. He sizes me up.

"What does he want?" he says.

"Hey, man, did you yam up all me bread?" the short officer asks.

"What do you keep accusing me for?" the tall officer says.

"Because I saw you last time when you did it. Do I go around and eat your food?"

"No."

"Then why don't you respect me?"

"What you jamming me up for? I said I didn't do it," the tall officer states.

"Gentlemen, I'm sorry to interrupt, but I was wondering if one of you can get Donny for me and we can be on our way."

"We don't take orders from you. You can pick him up after lunch," the officer replied.

"When's lunch?"

"Now!" the men say in unison.

Two hours later I am standing outside of the police station when Donny Moses walks out. He is not happy to see me, but at least he's free and today's incident is all behind him.

"Did you have anything to do with this?" he asks.

"Donny, listen, there are no easy answers," I say.

Donny holds up his hands and stops me. I can see in his eyes that he's trying to keep his anger at bay. I have to be delicate with my words.

"I've never spent a night in jail before, never—not until I had you as a client. In one week, my life has gone to hell, and I have you to thank for it."

Donny starts walking down the steps toward me. His fists are clenched, and his body language tells me I need to get out of the way. But I stand firm, and I pray that he will listen to reason.

"Hey, Donny, I'm sorry about this whole incident."

Donny walks up to me and plants his fist square in my jaw. I drop to one knee from the impact.

"Don't come anywhere near me or my business ever again! Do you understand?"

I give a head nod in agreement. I'm trying to shake off the sting of Donny's punch, but it's clear that I will be feeling the aftermath of that punch long after he has left. Donny keeps walking. I want to follow him and talk with him, but I'm afraid he will give me another stern warning.

Chapter Twenty

From the police station I went to Sammy's house. I figure he is the only Moses that will speak to me at this point. I don't know what I expect to come from this conversation, all I know is that I hope to clear the air and make something right, naïve as that may be, but it is the truth.

"I got some fresh trout I just finished cooking." Sammy opens the door for me.

I go inside the house and, as usual, Sammy has not bothered to clean. Newspapers and fishing gear cluttered all over the place, but the one place that is clean is his kitchen table. There are only two chairs, which confirms that Sammy doesn't get much company.

"Have a seat, Doc." Sammy points to one of the chairs.

I take a seat, and soon, Sammy places a plate of fresh fried fish in front of me. It smells good, and I'm sure it's delicious.

"So I hear you made a big stink of things," he says.

"That's a mild way of putting it." I take a bite into my fish. This meal is the highlight of my day.

"I want to thank you for getting my boy out."

"He shouldn't have been there to begin with, but your son already thanked me with his fist."

"He holds grudges. I tried to tell him that the longer he holds on to something, the heavier the weight."

I'm not someone who cries a lot. In fact, aside from my mother's funeral, I can count the number of times I've cried, but at this moment, I feel every emotion except for the tears.

"I know that look. I know that look very well, and I can tell, you will get through it."

"I pray that I will, but this is beyond me."

"Nothing is beyond God. I don't know what trouble you're in, but I know that if you keep pressing, you'll get through. It won't be easy, and it may take a huge sacrifice on your part, but you'll get through it."

"How can you be so sure?" I ask.

"Because one thing that I know to be true is that few men make their mistake going toward God. Their mistakes occur when they try to go *away* from Him."

Sammy is a flawed man, but so I am, sitting in his small kitchen eating fish. I felt a sense of hope that I could weather this storm. Maybe I can still turn things around.

For about an hour, Sammy and I play cards and share stories until we heard a weird sound coming from the side of his house.

"What's going on?" I say.

Sammy and I get up and walk over to the window. We see Donny Moses with a baseball bat in his hands, and he's taking swings at Sammy's boat.

"Lord have mercy!" Sammy runs outside, and I follow.

By the time we get to the side of the house where the boat is, Donny has already done a number on the boat. The windshields are broken, and the front end has also been damaged.

"Whoa, whoa, whoa! Son, what are you doing?"

"Seven years! Seven years! FAA inspections, maintenance, customs, and flying prima donnas around. Seven years—and my business is ruined all because of you," Donny points at Sammy, then he points at me, "and him. What am I supposed to do now?"

Donny takes a few more whacks at the boat, and though it pains Sammy to watch his life's work get destroyed, he didn't want to feel the wrath of his son. I didn't want to incur Donny's wrath either, but I couldn't let this father-and-son relationship become even more strained. As Donny picked up the bat to swing once again, I dart right in front of the boat.

"Enough," I say.

Anyone who claims that the eyes are not the window to a man's soul is a liar. I look into Donny's eyes and see rage that has built up to the point where he could take my head off at any moment's notice without hesitation.

"I'm sorry. Lord knows I didn't want any of this to happen. I'm trying to do the Lord's will."

Donny starts to chuckle, then his chuckle turns into a full-blown hysterical laugh.

"I don't know whose will you're doing, but it's not the Lord's."

"You're probably right, but what you're doing isn't God's will either."

I take a look at Sammy. His mouth is shut, and he is not uttering a word. I don't know if it's because of his son or the boat. I look back at Donny. He has now dropped his baseball stance, but the bat is still secure in his hands.

"You are father and son, and there is no logical reason why you two should be at odds with each other."

"Don't try to turn this around. This is about you and me."

"If it was just about you and me, then you wouldn't be here. You've held anger toward your father for years, and this is your opportunity to let the anger out."

My words cause Donny to drop his bat. At least I don't have to worry about my head being taken off, but I still had Donny's wrath to consider.

"I carried a whole lot of anger for my father and most of it was justified. But when he died, something happened. It doesn't take away all the hurt and pain of what my father caused, but when he died, it also took away the chance for a moment. I just wanted a moment when he and I were not enemies, but could actually be friends and maybe even father and son."

For the first time, father and son made eye contact. Thank God for small miracles.

"Let me be clear, this beef between you and me has nothing to do with the money you squandered. It has *everything* to do with you never wanting to take responsibility for your actions," Donny says.

"Me?" Sammy has a legitimate look of shock plastered over his face.

"Yes, you. Even now, you still don't take responsibility for what happened between you and Mom."

Donny mentioning his mother turns an otherwise easygoing Sammy furious. Sammy takes off his baseball cap and rubs his head. I guess he's trying to figure out how to respond to his son's claim.

"You know, for a smart man, you have a short memory. The day I left, do you remember that?" Sammy says.

"Of course, I remember. I was thirteen. How could I forget?"

"I took you to the park, remember? We tossed the football around, and then afterward, we sat on the bleachers and talked."

"I remember all of this. What's the point?" Donny asks.

"I don't regret marrying your mother. If not for her, there would be no you. I bring up that moment, because even on one of the worst days of my life, I still wouldn't have traded it away. Playing football with you still made my life worth living."

Donny puts his head down and wipes his face. He doesn't want to show emotions in front of his father.

"I'm sorry. I didn't know how to say it until now," Sammy says.

"Don't miss your moment," I tell Donny.

These two have a lot to talk about, and they don't need me there as they hash things out. I start to walk away.

"Where are you going? This isn't over," Donny says.

"You're right, it's not. I got to make things right first."

I keep walking because in a few hours I have a party to attend and tycoon to bring down.

Chapter Twenty-one

When I packed for this trip, I packed a light jacket because the nights on the island are warm. Tonight, I need a suit, and since the only suit I have is the one I bought earlier, I decide to wear it again. Tonight, I will uncover the reason why Pastor Cole was murdered . . . one way or another. Randall Knott perceives me to be a man of value, and I must keep up that appearance.

A sleek boat splits the waves wide open as it jets toward the dock. It's not easy to spot this boat in the cloak of night. As the boat approaches, nerves start to build up in the pit of my stomach. I don't know what I will have to do tonight, but I pray that the Lord will see me through an otherwise impossible situation.

The boat pulls into the dock, and I realize that there is no turning back now.

"Minister Nicodemus Dungy?" the Haitian driver asks.

"Yes. I'm Minister Dungy."

"Mr. Knott is expecting your company. Right this way, sir."

After a little hesitation, I finally decide to step onto the boat. I won't find out anything staying home.

"Compliments of Mr. Knott." The driver points to a bottle of champagne and caviar.

I'm not a fan of either, but as we cruise along the ocean, it's hard to imagine a better way to enjoy the evening. Of course, for me, it's Victory. She would have loved being in the boat headed to a black tie affair.

We cruise along in utter blackness for fifteen minutes until I start to see a light. The closer we travel toward it, the brighter the light gets. It can serve as a beacon to any vessel lost at sea. A few minutes more of travel and the structure starts to take shape. This must be our destination because the building is a mansion with Greek pillars, which is signature Randall Knott. It's clear Randall has more money than he knows what to do with it. The man owns two mansions on the same island, one at the top of the hill and one at the bottom. I guess he chose to ditch the traditional Christmas lighting in exchange for regular bright lights.

The boat pulls into the port, and there is a cute Haitian girl waiting for me with a clipboard.

"Name?" she asks.

"Nicodemus Dungy." I flash her my passport.

The young lady scans her clipboard until she arrives at my name. "Enjoy your evening, Mr. Dungy."

"Thank you very much."

I walk up the dock toward the house. I could have sworn I was walking into heaven with how bright the house is and how vibrant the music is. As I enter the home, to the left is a banquet-size dining room, and to the right is a dance floor with a twelve-piece band. It must be an unwritten rule that if you are rich, then you must have two winding staircases in your home.

I wasn't hungry, so I walk over to the ballroom and watch as the couples danced. They were doing the Viennese Waltz which reminds me of my mother, the dance instructor. I used to think that the dance was boring; I didn't realize how graceful the dance truly is and the need to be graceful.

"Want to dance, handsome?"

I turn around. To my surprise there stands Maggie Fuller. She hails from Texas and was the wife of the

former governor. Fuller is an heiress to the oil tycoon
James Fuller. Even with her divorce, Fuller is still very
much influential in the political world. If a candidate
wanted to win the middle-aged white women's vote, they
would need both Maggie's money and influence.

"It would be an honor." I take Ms. Fuller by the hand,
and we begin to waltz.

"First time I'm seeing you at one of these events," she
says.

"First I was invited to one."

"Well, I know this much, you're not a politician," Ms.
Fuller says before I spin her around.

"What gave me away?"

"You have this aura of a civil servant."

"I thought that's what a politician is."

"Don't be silly, darling. Every politician says he is a
civil servant because the truth is too much for the voters
to bear." She leans into my ear. "The truth is that they are
addicted to power."

Ms. Fuller giggles as if she just let me in on an earth-shat-
tering secret. Truth is, Ms. Fuller is not telling me something
I don't already know, but I'll play the game nonetheless.

We dance until the end of the song, and then I bow to
Ms. Fuller, who happens to be a pretty good dancer, and
I got a chance to relive my youth. As I exit the ballroom, I
see another servant with his eyes dead set on me.

"Mr. Dungy, Mr. Knott requests your presence at once."

"Certainly." I turn to Ms. Fuller and shake her hand. "It
was an honor, Ms. Fuller."

"Hon, the pleasure was all mine," she says.

I follow the servant up the stairs through a long, dark
hallway. The rest of the house is lit up, but this part of
the house is dark. It's dark so that none of the guests can
wonder off upstairs unless they are being escorted by
one of Knott's servants. I'm starting to think that this is a

game of Clue. After the long hallway, we then made sharp turns to the right, then down another hallway, and then a turn to the left before descending down a set of stairs where a door sits on the opposite end of the stairs.

The servant opens the door, and cigar smoke greets me as I walk into the room. Once inside, I realize that the *real* party was happening within this room. All of the pastors from the conference except Pastor Bryant are in attendance. Some were smoking cigars, others were enjoying the young ladies who pranced around in their lingerie. I guess this is how members of the Cloth unwind. They are too caught up in their own decadence to notice that an outsider was in their mix.

I walk over to the bar and pour myself a brandy. I'm in a room full of wolves that left their sheep's clothing at the door. I wish a scene like this disturbed me, but it doesn't. Over the years, I've grown cold, and there are very few things that surprise me now.

"What are you doing here?"

I turn around, and there stands Pastor Jackson, only he doesn't have a smile on his face like he did the last time.

"Knott invited me."

"Knott's out of his mind inviting you. You're not even a member."

I take a good hard swallow of my brandy. "Do you think Knott cares anything about your organization?"

"Of course not. There's not a single person in here that thinks Knott has our best interests at heart. His concern is with lining his own pockets, and as long as he lines mine and this organization's, then we are cool."

"What about saving souls and preaching the Gospel? Has that gotten lost in the business of making money?" I ask.

"Not for a second. One of the main complaints about the church is how it's always asking people for money.

Now, those same people don't have problems dropping their children off at day care or having a free meal during the holidays, but let us ask them to help out, and all of sudden, they want to call us crooks. The Cloth generates enough income through our various enterprises to help keep our ministries thriving."

"It sounds too good to be true. What's the catch?" I ask.

"There is no catch. You see how the members worship the leaders as if they were Jesus Himself. That kind of pressure would crush a lesser man. I protect my brothers. I don't exploit them."

"I'm sure you don't . . . for a handsome fee," I say.

"And like you do your work for free? When is the last time you got a check postmarked from heaven? It takes money to change lives, and you of all people should know that."

"I guess." I start to scan the room to see who else has been invited to this meeting.

"You know, we both have common interests. If you want to be a part of the Cloth, I can pull some strings."

Before I can answer Pastor Jackson's question with an empathic "no," a set of double doors opens up, and Randall Knott enters in a black tuxedo with a cigar and a drink in his hands.

"Gentlemen, thank you for waiting. If you wouldn't mind following me into the next room we can begin our presentation." Knott holds up his hands. "Not to worry, these lovely ladies will be waiting for you when we get back."

The men laugh, and then follow Knott into the next room. I trail behind the rest of the men, and as soon as I walk through the door, another assistant closes the door and shuts all of us in.

"Gentlemen, thank you for coming. I know that's it sad to lose a brother and a business partner like Pastor Cole.

Why don't we have a moment of silence to remember him?"

Every man bows his head, including Knott. Knott doesn't strike me as a religious man, but a shrewd businessman who will adapt to his environment to ensure his bottom line. If we were all rabbis, he would probably have a yarmulke on his head.

"Well, I thank you again, and I know that it's rough, but what I have to show you will be well worth it."

Randall walks behind a table that has a sheet over it. He pulls back the sheet like a magician revealing a trick. It's a replica of Crystal Cove, only there is a huge hotel in the corner of the island.

"I present Paradise Towers' Hotel and Casino. This will be the premiere destination on Crystal Cove," Knott says.

The other men in the room were amazed while I was repulsed.

"We are talking about a five-star resort with quality gambling and a beautiful view. All I ask from you gentlemen is half a million dollars per member buy in and you will, in return, receive a take of the house."

"How are you planning to pay out our profits?" one minister asked.

"The same as usual, through Cayman accounts that will be established through shell corporations."

The men start to nod their heads in agreement. A hotel casino on an island is a great way to make a profit.

"How long would it take for it to be built?" Pastor Jackson asks.

"I have all the permits and paperwork drawn up, and we will break ground soon. My guess, within two years we will open the doors. You, gentlemen, would have a free suite available whenever you are in town."

The men are nodding their heads in agreement once again. There's no way that any of these men invest in a casino in Vegas or Atlantic City; too much exposure. On a small island, however, they can operate under the radar.

"Two years seems like a long time to get a return on our investment, and a casino seems too risky."

"I know it's a gamble." Knott laughs at his own bad joke. "But in all seriousness, the reason why you guys are silent partners is so that the public will not get wind of your investment. But think about the things you can do with the money that will come rolling in from this casino once it opens."

"What about Pastor Cole?" another member asks. "Was he on board?"

That question brought a sour look to Knott's face. He could handle any question that these so-called leaders were asking except for the obvious proverbial elephant in the room.

"Listen, fellas, full disclosure," Knott says as he put his cigar out in a nearby crystal ashtray.

He puts his head down like he's going to make a full confession to the murder of Pastor Cole. He then looks up and starts to blink his eyes as if to fight back the tears. I guess it's hard for the devil to cry on cue.

"We've benefited a great deal from our business endeavors," Knott says.

The members in the room start to nod and mumble in agreement. I'm the only reserved one of the bunch that's not buying this act.

"You know the locals here have a saying. When someone is being greedy, they call that person 'big-eyed.' Well, there's no simple way to put it, but that's what the case was for Pastor Cole."

Incredible, not only did Knott have the audacity to make such an erroneous claim, but the men in the room bought it, hook, line, and sinker. This is the closest thing to an out-of-body experience I have ever felt.

"You gentlemen voted him as your leader, so I proposed this deal to him first. He wanted to cut you guys out of the deal for a bigger piece for himself. I rejected his offer because that was the right thing to do. Now what happened to Cole was tragic, and Lord knows what other deals he was involved in, but may God rest his soul."

The whole room has become ablaze with chatter about Cole and his supposed "side deal" with Knott. I don't buy it, and I think that Pastor Cole might have rejected Knott's proposal.

"And, brothers, this is too good of a deal not to let you get a chance to invest. Just think of the people you can help with this money," Knott says.

A closer look at the model and I realize that Randall Knott plans to break ground on the land where Janae's house sits, which means she is all that is standing in his way.

"Then why is *he* here?" Pastor Jackson points directly at me.

For the first time, the gentlemen realize that I'm in the room, and they start to become nervous. Shows you how quick things can change. A minute ago, Pastor Jackson offered me a membership into the Cloth. Now he has just thrown me under the bus.

"I have retained his services to help make sure that all of our business transactions see the light of day."

I wasn't aware that I have even accepted an offer, or been offered one, but that's neither here nor there, I guess. I now know what Randall Knott is planning with the Cloth. I now know why Pastor Cole was killed, and I now need to get to Janae before she's next on the list.

Chapter Twenty-two

I am in a daze on the boat ride back from Knott's home. I can't believe that this group of so-called men of God are getting into bed with Randall Knott to build a casino. Lord knows how many bribes and threats Randall had to lay out in order to put this venture in play. None of these men who called themselves Pastor Cole's friend were even disgusted by the business proposal. All they see is dollar signs in their greed, and they plan to take from their churches' tithes and offerings to fulfill their greed. Of course, greed is an insatiable desire.

"Are you sure that this is where you want to stop?" my driver asks.

I snap out of my trance and see Janae's home coming into the horizon. I need to warn her.

"Yes, just for a brief moment I need to see someone," I say.

The boat pulls up to the dock, and this time I don't have to jump out and swim. Janae's house still looks like a jack o' lantern, but I'm not worried about that now. My main concern is getting her to leave before something happens to her. I hop out of the boat and make my way to the house. A shadowy figure moves out to the front door.

"Minister, didn't expect to see you. You want me to tell you your future?"

If she didn't see me coming, I doubt she can tell my future.

"I'm not interested in any of that foolishness. I'm here to warn you. Randall Knott plans to build a hotel casino right on your land, and I'm afraid he'll stop at nothing to do it."

It was as if I didn't say anything. Janae turns around and goes inside the house.

"You need to leave," I say as I enter the house behind her.

"Oh no, death is coming, and it don't matter where I go; it'll find me."

I walk over to her table, and it looks like she's been playing with her tarot cards again. This time, she has the fool, judgment, and death cards laid out.

"It doesn't have to find you tonight. I have a boat outside. You can come with me, and we can figure something out."

"You'd be the smartest man in the world if you can figure out how to outsmart death," Janae says. "Many men try to outrun death, and they end up right into him."

I'm not in the mood for Janae's spooky talk. I need her to come with me until I can figure this whole thing out. "We need to go, now!"

Janae doesn't respond. Instead, she just picks up the picture of her two boys. She smiles, and her smile is not sadistic, but endearing.

"What happened to them?"

"The devil got to them, that's what. I lost one of them years ago."

Janae turns around and smiles at me. "He came twice."

I'm confused about whom she's referring to, and the look on my face must've conveyed it.

"Your friend the preacher. The first time he called himself trying to get me saved, when all the while he was trying to get me to accept Knott's deal. The second time was different; he was different. He apologized and told me not to sell. Then the next day, he was dead."

A cold chill swept over me at the grim details. In our first encounter, Janae did not mention to me that Pastor Cole visited her twice.

"Go on now; Janae is going to be all right."

"I can't leave you here." I try to grab her arm, but she fights back.

"You can't make me go either. Go. Be the man that you are and don't worry about little old me."

"You're just going to sit here and await your fate?" I couldn't make sense of Janae's logic.

"You should learn to do the same."

There is nothing I can say that would cause Janae to leave her home. I stand there for a minute trying to think of something I could say that will cause this woman to fight for her survival. Self-preservation is a common trait in the United States, but not for Janae. She will not be moved, and so I turn to walk out of her house. Before I leave Janae and walk back to the boat I pray that I'm wrong on my assessment of Knott.

"Is everything all right, sir?" the driver asks.

"No, no, it's not, but there's nothing we can do about it now. We just have to let things play out," I say.

"Excuse me, sir?" the driver asks.

"Nothing, I'm sorry. I was just thinking out loud."

Or maybe I'm still praying out loud, hoping that God hears me and will show grace and mercy to Janae. I also pray that I'm wrong and that Janae's life is not in danger. I get into the boat and disappear in the night.

The next morning as I wake up, I do something I haven't done since my arrival at the island. I turned on the TV. I guess I need to escape the worries of Janae and the death of Pastor Cole. I flip several channels until I arrived at a station that was playing a Pastor Cole sermon. What are the odds?

"Most people got this whole prosperity thing wrong, and I admit that I have, over the years, played a part in the misconception."

I wonder if this is a recent sermon.

"Prosperity in the Kingdom of God means that God is with you in every aspect of your life. It means that you trust God wholeheartedly in every aspect of your life, and your faithfulness produces fruit."

Janae is right. Pastor Cole had changed, and it's tragic that the world didn't get a chance to benefit from this change.

After the program, I went downstairs. Once again, Sammy and Adele are downstairs drinking coffee and talking. Only their conversation didn't seem lighthearted.

"Why the sad faces?" I ask.

"Not sad, just shocked," Adele says.

"What's going on?"

"Demetrius and his mother Janae were found dead this morning," Sammy says.

My heart drops at the news. I just saw Janae last night, and this morning, she's gone. Randall Knott just killed two more people, and I can't help but to feel partly responsible for it.

Chapter Twenty-three

I borrow Sammy's truck and take the road that leads to Demetrius's house. He survives being shot and almost drowns, only to have his life taken from him at a moment's notice. I know not many people are going to shed a tear over his death, but it bothers me. No matter how deplorable of an individual he was, Demetrius was still a human being, and if he died without knowing Jesus and the power of His redemptive work, then the eternity that awaits Demetrius is far worse.

Demetrius's death does play a major shift in a larger, more disturbing narrative: someone is killing off anyone in connection with Pastor Cole's murder. That means everyone, including myself, could be a target. I know that it's someone that has been hired by Randall Knott, and there is enough separation between the assassin and Knott for plausible deniability.

I drive past the Dixon household. Both of their cars are in the driveway, which means that they either patched things up, or Mrs. Dixon has chosen to keep her affair a secret. I remember when the only thing that was impeding on my vacation was the affair between Prophet Chambers and Mrs. Dixon. How I wish I could trade problems. I know one thing: Victory would still be here if I had never taken on this job, now my life, as well as Adele's and Sammy's, are at risk.

I arrive at the top of the hill where Demetrius's house is located. The door is wide open, and there are several cars parked between the driveway and the door. I see people running in and out of his house with flat-screen TVs, cigar boxes, and clothes. I don't see any smoke, so there isn't a fire. I get out of the car and start walking toward the front door. The man who drove me up to Demetrius's place the other night comes out with a silver case.

"What's going on?" I ask.

"Demetrius is dead."

"I know, but what are you doing?"

"The police and the feds will be here to raid this place. Me and the guys are getting what's owed to us. You'll need to hurry up," the driver says.

According to reports, Demetrius died at the hospital so that doesn't make his house a crime scene, at least not yet. The driver didn't wait for my reply. He hightailed it to the truck he picked me up in and left with the case in hand. Who knows what is in that case, but it's enough for the driver to bypass the rest of the spoils. Demetrius once considered himself invincible and ruled with fear. It didn't take long for his people to get over their fears and take what they felt belongs to them.

I walk into house and feel like I'm watching the Rodney King riot all over again. There are people running all over the place with items from the house in their hands. Jewelry—you name it—trying to pack as much stuff away before the authorities arrive to cart off the rest.

I walk over to the living room. Everything except for the furniture has been taken. Demetrius had several plants in his living room. All of them have been turned over and the vases broken. I walk over to the kitchen counter and there is a bottle of Hennessy Beauté du Siècle. The fact that it's still here is odd. Beauté du Siècle is one of the most expensive Cognacs in the world. I would have to clean out my bank account just to buy one bottle. I think the bottle must've just been opened because even though it is almost full, there is glass of the Hennessy next to it. I lean in to get a whiff, and I detect that there is nothing that would suggest poison, but how else can someone take Demetrius out?

There are plenty of poisons that are odorless and tasteless, but in order to deliver this lethal bottle to Demetrius and get him to drink it, it would have to be someone he trusts, and there's only one person I know on this island who Demetrius would trust.

I didn't even know Sammy's pickup truck is capable of going over eighty-five miles per hour, until I race along on an uneven road. I now have two theories. Either Elisha Davis is the killer, and she has been playing me this whole time, or she's next on the real killer's list. The only way I will know which theory is true is by going to her house.

I am coming up on Elisha's house now, and I realize that I don't have a gun on me. I don't have time to stop by Adele's place and pick up the gun she gave me earlier either.

I pull up to Elisha's house. The door is cracked open. I look around my surroundings to make sure that I'm not walking into an ambush. I then step inside the house. The house doesn't looked ransacked, but it there are some things missing. A few pictures are missing, and the door to the bedroom is open.

I walk into the bedroom and check to make sure there are no would-be assailants hiding in the corners. The closet is open and clothes are missing and strewn on the floor. Clothes seem to be missing from the dresser as well. Whether she is the killer or not is irrelevant at this point. Elisha is gone.

I walk back into the living room and notice that on the floor lay two pictures. The first is a picture of the Eiffel Tower.

That is a message from Elisha to me, that she escaped. I hope she enjoys Paris around this time of the year, and I hope she makes her family proud. The second picture is the same picture that Janae had in her house. It is a picture of Demetrius and his brother. There is a connection there. A message that Elisha was trying to convey to someone, maybe even me. But I don't know, and I can't make sense of two people who are dead and one person who is missing. I need to go somewhere to think.

Chapter Twenty-four

The news of Janae's and Demetrius's deaths, and Elisha's sudden disappearance drives me to the one place where I know I can find answers, or at least pour my heart out. I go to the same church that Sammy took me to the last few weeks. Prayer changes things. That's an elementary principle in Christianity, but within it, there's truth. I thought I would find myself alone, but I'm alone, Pastor Clayborn is here, and she is praying up a storm.

Physically, she's the only one in the room, but spiritually, she has a captive audience with her prayer. Pastor Clayborn is a true prayer warrior, and her prayers have somewhat become legendary in Crystal Cove. I hear stories of people who are fatally ill and how they make a miraculous recovery thanks to her prayers.

"Thank you, Jesus! You are all I need. Anything that's not you is not worth it. You are worthy to be praised. You inhabit the praises of your people, Jesus, and I thank you," she says.

I feel moved to fall to my knees right there in the back pew. I close my eyes and clasp my hands. For a minute, my mind is like a congested freeway; too much going on to settle down and focus. Then I start to settle down and remind myself why I am here. I am here to connect the dots as far as this case goes. I'm here searching for a spiritual epiphany. Despite my best efforts, all of my human efforts have failed, and here I am at ground zero.

"Thank you, Jesus, for your grace and your mercy. Father, I thank you for making a way out of no way," I say.

I can't even hear the pastor any more. I can't even make out what I'm saying, and I don't care. All I know is it feels like a fog has lifted, and my mind has started to clear up.

This whole mystery lies before me and the pieces are starting to connect in ways I haven't even imagined. There is Janae and the two boys in the picture; Randall Knott and the casino; Elisha and her relationship to Pastor Cole; Pastor Cole and his relationship to the Cloth; and the power struggle between Demetrius and Randall Knott. Everything starts to come together and tells an unbelievable story right to the end.

"I know who killed them!" I say. These words came out of my prayer with sweat pouring from my pores.

"What are you talking about?" Clayborn says.

She is standing behind me, which means she must've concluded her prayer. I stand up with my knees feeling sore.

"How long have I been praying?"

"At least two hours. Boy, you were shouting it down. Yeah, there's a power that dwells within these walls. I've seen the Holy Spirit do some amazing things here."

No argument there. The Holy Spirit has done an amazing work in my life in the last two hours. God is neither a respecter of persons nor a respecter of churches. Wherever His name is being lifted up, God dwells in the midst.

Panic set in as I realize where the killer may be headed next. I reach into my pocket and speed dial Adele's home. She doesn't have a cell phone, only a house phone. No answer after about a dozen rings . . . until her voice mail comes on.

"Adele, this is Nic. I pray that you are out somewhere, but if you're not and you're listening to this message, get out of the house! Now! I'll explain later. Go somewhere safe."

"Boy, what's wrong with you?" Pastor asks as I hang up the phone.

"Nothing. Everything is right if the Lord can let me do this one thing," I say.

Pastor Clayborn is confused by what I say but no matter, I know what I need to do and where I need to go next.

Chapter Twenty-five

If I was in L.A., the police would be chasing me and a news helicopter would be flying over me. Thank God I'm not in L.A. The main road for Crystal Cove only has two lanes, but I swerve in and out of both, trying to get to Adele's house as fast as possible. I dodge oncoming cars and trucks. Lord knows I have made quite a few enemies today with my driving alone, but I don't care. I believe the killer has been tying up loose ends, which mean I'm next on the list. I can't afford for Adele to be a causality of this war between Demetrius and Knott.

"Move out of the way!" I honk my horn at the truck in front of me, but it continues to drive slowly.

The bed of the truck is filled with car parts and other junk that I can't make out, but what's bothersome is that the items hanging off the truck have created a blind spot for me, so I continue to swerve in and out.

"Come on . . . move!" I honk again, but to no avail.

I decide to try to swerve around and get in front of the truck. When I switch to the next lane, sure enough, there is an oncoming car and the space between me and the car is small.

"Lord Jesus," I say as I speed up and cut in front of the truck before I crash into the oncoming car.

The truck that is now behind me honks his horn as I take the exit that leads to Adele's house and the truck speeds down the hill. I thank God that the truck Sammy let me borrow has enough juice in it to get to her house.

I'm sure I will owe Sammy a new vehicle after today . . . *if* I even survive today. I get out of the car and race up to the porch and throw open the door.

"Adele!" I yell as I enter the kitchen. No one is here.

I go from room to room and I neither hear nor see anything. I go back in the living room and try to figure out my next play. There is no sign of blood or of a struggle, which means Adele is alive, thank God, and more importantly, she is gone. Now that I'm alone waiting for the killer to show up, I need a plan of attack.

The living room and the kitchen are too open. The killer can take me out without even stepping foot into the house. Upstairs will be my best option, but I can't go upstairs empty-handed.

I walk out of the living room down the hall to the room where Adele keeps all of her husband's memories. Adele brought me into this room to share a very private moment with her. She shared her husband's wonderful, but dark, legacy. She also showed me his array of weapons, and I will need one of his guns to stand a fighting chance. I try to turn the knob, but the door is locked. I should've known that it will be locked, but that goes to show where my head is at the present moment.

I run upstairs. Again, I don't see any sign of Adele, nor do I see any signs of blood or a struggle. Still thanking God for Adele not being home, that just leaves the killer and me. I go into my room and look out the window. If my theory is correct, then the killer is going to arrive by boat.

I stare outside for an hour with my eyes focused on the dock. During that hour I play the game of "what-ifs." *What if I never came to Crystal Cove? What if I passed on Pastor Bryant's offer?* I guess I wouldn't be in the position I am currently in now, sitting and waiting for my death. I bow my head and clasp my hands.

"Father, you have been good to me. I thank you for my life and each moment I have lived. I know that every memory, including the bad ones, was to help shape me into a better man. Forgive me, Father, for all of the times I fell short or lost my way. In the end, I love you, and I just wanted to do your will. I pray that you see that in Jesus' name, amen."

I stare out the window for at least another ten minutes before I see a speedboat heading toward shore. The boat pulls against the dock and a person hops out. I turn around with my heart racing. I was right—I was right!

I realize that I am about to die, and at this moment I have developed a new power. I'm not talking about powers like X-men; no. I'm talking about a higher sense of the world within me and the world around me. My senses are so keen that I wonder why they haven't kicked in until now.

Take, for example, the view from my room. Every day for the last two weeks I have walked out onto the terrace of my room and gazed at the ocean. I have only been able to see so far, but today, I can almost see the nearest island next to the one I am currently on. I can smell the saltwater from the sea and feel the wind race through my skin. I pour myself a glass of scotch without ice. I know for a fact that it cools as much as it burns while going down. Of course, I haven't had a sip, and it's not like I haven't recently had a drink, but still, there is something to be said about going to meet my Savior having at least challenged my darkest demon. I stare at the glass for what feels like eternity before I set the glass back down on my desk. Even though I am about to die, and I'm certain that I won't lose my salvation over a drink, I still can't take a drink; not now, not anymore.

I spend a good portion of my life delving in secrets and entertaining the demon elixir. As a result, there aren't too many things that I am proud of in my life. No amount of alcohol could drown out my problems, I see that now, but I also see my end. What's one last drink? I know I said that I wouldn't, but I can't resist.

I pick up the glass and bring the scotch to my nose. It's a decent scotch, but I've had better. It will have to do though. I take the drink, and it satisfies my thirst. Lord, forgive me for being weak and flawed in my hour of temptation.

Since I have already given into one temptation, I take in my other vice. I pick up the pack of smokes I have on my table and place one cigarette on the edge of my lips.

I savor the taste of the tobacco for a minute before I strike a match that I picked up from the Atlantis Casino. I couldn't resist making a stop along the way to Crystal Cove.

I protect the flame with my hands from the island breeze as I draw it in close and light the end of my cigarette. I take in the smoke before I release it into the wind. The day is clear, and the ocean is inviting. It's a good place God picked for me to die.

At least I will die a millionaire, though I didn't get the chance to spend the money. And what's the point? No one knows about the money except my employer. I wish I could give to charity or to Victory, another thing on my list of regrets.

Any moment now, my killer will arrive. It won't be long now . . . last call. I think about Victory and the last time I saw her. Her eyes were full of disappointment, and it was well deserved. I was rotten to her, and I took something that was special and ruined it. I did it to myself. There is so much I want to tell her, and I can't now. I guess my final lesson before I check out is that I should say the things that I need to say when I have the time to say it. Oh well, what good does regret do for me now? It can't make me bulletproof.

The door clicks open. The hardwood floors snitches on my assailant. It's almost that time. Now my heart is more scared than my mind.

I have to take a deep breath and remain calm. This person may take my life, but they won't take my pride. I won't give them the satisfaction.

The door to my office creaks open.

"I know who you are," I say with my back turned. "I know everything, and I know why you killed him."

I turn around to face my murderer. It turns out to be the person who I suspected. I am right. Boy, how I hate being right, especially now when I am about to die. I hope the information I left will be enough to see this person brought to justice. Now a smirk stretches across my assailant's face, and a 9 mm gun points at my temple. Here we go.

"Are you surprised it's me, fam?" Cameron says.

Cameron is the other boy in the picture next to his brother, Demetrius. I take a long drag of the cigarette and let the smoke flow out of my mouth. "No, not at all. I figured it out that it was you a long time ago."

Yeah, I know that's a lie, but the last thing I want is for this little knucklehead to think he outsmarted me.

"Quit lying. Cameron outsmarted everybody. I know I did."

"Well, the one good thing about my death, aside from being with Jesus, of course, is that I won't have to hear you refer to yourself in third person any longer."

Cameron lets out a smirk. He holds all the cards, and he knows that all I'm trying to do is goad him into making a mistake.

"You know your mother kept two pictures of you and your brother Demetrius. In fact, Demetrius told me right before he died that he actually owned the land that your house sits on. It was passed down from generation to generation."

"Mr. Knott offered us millions for that land, and he wouldn't sell—saying he didn't want to ruin our legacy. Saying he didn't need his money—but what about me? What about Cameron? I don't make any money, and he doesn't do a thing for his own brother."

"So you make a deal with the devil. First, you kill Pastor Cole for trying to talk your mother out of selling the house. You knew your mother and brother wouldn't sell, so finally you had to kill them too. Your own flesh and blood—at least Cain didn't kill Eve."

"For $3 million, yeah, I'll kill a crazy old lady and a selfish wannabe gangster. I don't care if they were my mother and brother. I'll kill whoever Mr. Knott wants me to kill."

"Is he paying you extra to kill me?" I ask.

"You should've left it alone, fam. I don't know what you did, but Mr. Knott is going to pay me a hundred thousand to kill you."

Nice to see my life is worth a hundred thousand to Knott. I know people who would wipe out their whole family reunion for $3 million, but not me. I often wonder how much hatred can one human being stomach to drive him to kill his own family.

"You're a pretty smart dude, Mr. Dungy. I hate that I have to do this." Cameron readjusts his stance.

Father, forgives me and into your arms I go, and if possible, rather through a dream or a vision, and convey to Victory that I love her and that I'm sorry.

I heard the sound of a shotgun being racked; the interesting thing is that Cameron has a .45 with a silencer on it. He turns around, and there is Adele with a shotgun pointed at Cameron's lower body.

"Now, baby, I'm going to need you to put the gun down and get up out my house now," Adele says calmly.

"Please, old lady, that gun is bigger than you. You'll probably fly down the stairs if you try to fire it."

"Are you willing to bet your life on that?" she asks.

Cameron is distracted, and without hesitation, I step to the left side of his gun and lift his arm up. He fires a shot, and when his eyes lock on me, I punch him square in his nose. The punch causes him to lose his grip. I take the gun and smack him on the side of his forehead with the gun and knock him out.

"Are you okay?" I ask Adele.

"No, no, I'm not. I come home to watch *Dr. Oz,* and I almost had to shoot a fool in my guest room, and now I got a hole in my roof."

I know it may not be appropriate, but I start to laugh hysterically, and I don't even stop myself. Eventually Adele stops looking at me crazy and joins in on the laughter.

The police carry Cameron off in the squad car. Adele should feel proud; she has the same amount of police presence as Pastor Cole had when he was murdered. This island has been stirred up enough over the last week. I stand on the porch after the police have questioned me. I'll have to go down to the station for more questioning, but for right now, the police will give me time. I need to adjust to the fact that I had a gun pointed in my face less than an hour ago.

Sammy comes over as soon as he hears the news to comfort Adele and me. It's great to have familiar faces around.

"Darn shame Knott hired that boy to kill his own family," Sammy says.

"It's a shame that I can't prove that Knott was behind it."

"Knott?" Adele asks.

I start to pace the porch with my hands in my pocket. There are so many angles I'm turning over in my head.

"Randall Knott was trying to purchase the land that Janae's house sits on. Demetrius was trying to stop him, and Knott hired Cameron to take them both out. Janae was both Demetrius and Cameron's mother," I say.

"There were whispers, but Janae would dismiss them," Adele says.

I look at Adele and Sammy. They are both visibly shocked. I guess the island isn't an open book. Demetrius and Janae kept their family connection a secret. Impressive.

"So what are you going to do now?" Sammy asks.

"I may not be able to prove that Knott had Pastor Cole killed, but that doesn't mean I'm going to let him go free."

After the police leave, I go upstairs and hop on Adele's computer. I need to do some research, and I need to get in contact with my friend Paul from the *Times*. Knott probably thinks that I'm dead. I've been trying to figure out why he would want to have me killed, and the best conclusion I can gather is that I know too much, and I didn't prove to be a real asset. Plus, I'm sure that some of the members of the Cloth threatened to withdraw their investment in the casino if Knott brought me on board. In retrospect, it was an easy decision for Knott to make and for Cameron to carry out.

After awhile, the Internet finally comes up. I start to research as much information as I can find on Knott and his corporation. To my delight, I discover that Knott owns a lot of businesses in Miami. The information available online shows that Knott is chairman of the board, his golden boy Douglas Madison is the vice president of Knott Corp. Miami operations. I wonder if he knows about his boss and all of his business dealings. I'm going to have to find out.

I leave a message for Paul to call me back with all the information he can find on Douglas Madison, and I promise him that his research will be worth it. Next, I'm going to need to book a flight. Donny Moses isn't the only charter pilot in town. He's just the best. However, I doubt he'll let me near his plane again. In any case, I need to leave the island today, if possible.

I start to pack. Even in a rush, I'm still very systematic in how I fold my clothes and put them in their numerous compartments. At least with me leaving, Adele and Sammy will not be in danger any longer. It's not easy being my friend, and I see the type of strain that I put on my relationships. Maybe before it's all said and done, I'll find a way to better appreciate those close to me.

"You're leaving?" Adele asks.

I stop packing and notice that Adele seems sad to see me leaving. I could've sworn that she would want me gone as soon as possible. I was just someone looking for a place to stay on the beach, and I gained so much more from my time with her than she with me.

"I have to go, Adele. I have to finish this."

"You won't be satisfied until they put a bullet in your head."

"They tried to put a bullet in my head. I'm not going to give them another opportunity."

Adele's eyes get sadder. I guess she's seen that look before in a man and heard these same words. Her husband continued to fight a war that had long ended. I'm fighting a war that seems pointless to her. I wish I could make her understand, but I don't have the time.

"I can't thank you enough for your hospitality, and I promise I'll be back to visit you," I say.

"I'm going to hold you to that promise now," Adele says. She then lets out a little smile.

There's a knock on the door, and it's Sammy, who has made his way upstairs. Adele gives him a smile, and he walks in.

"Are you leaving, Doc?" Sammy asks.

"Yeah, I have a few loose ends to tie up."

I start to pack again before I realize that Sammy has his hands on Adele's shoulders, and she is not elbowing him; nor is she threatening to hurt him. The threat on my life must've made me delusional.

"Is there something you want to tell me?" I ask Adele.

"No, just mind your own business now. That's what your problem is—you stay in other folks' business," she says.

"Yeah, you need to stop hating," Sammy says.

We all have a good laugh, and that is something I need. I am a firm believer in the scriptures, and laughter is medicine to the soul. The fact that I can laugh means that there is hope, and hope does not disappoint.

"You take care of yourself now," Adele says.

I give her a hug, and I shake Sammy's hand. "Thanks again."

This isn't a good-bye, but for now I have to bring Knott to justice. No matter what Knott has done, it has not escaped God, and he hasn't escaped me. I'm about to book a flight to Miami, and I plan to take Knott down.

Chapter Twenty-six

When I told Donny Moses that I was leaving the island, he did not hesitate to fly me from Crystal Cove to Fort Lauderdale. My destination is about an hour outside Miami. Donny assures me that the airport in Fort Lauderdale is less congested than Miami International. I take his word for it. From the airport I rent a car and drive out to Miami. My first stop is Southwest Christian Center. I need to see about a friend.

Here's a fun fact. I've been to Miami at least a dozen times, and I have yet to visit South Beach and other famous parts of the city. Unfortunately, I'm certain that the streak will not be broken today, for this is an all-business trip.

I arrive at Southwest Christian Center. The church is a warehouse that has been converted and extended upon its original design. Thanks to a savvy design of the front of the building with a huge cross, no one ever gives the building a second look. It's a weekday, and there are just a few cars in the parking lot, but there is one person I can count on to be at the church, rain or shine.

"Vinnie!" I say as Vinnie opens the door for me.

Vinnie is half Italian and half Puerto Rican. It's a long story; the main thing is Vinnie is well connected.

"Nic, it's been too long. How have you been?" Vinnie gives me a hug and lets me inside the church lobby.

"It's been too long, Vinnie. How's the family?"

"Tony's in high school. Kid's got quite an arm. He's going to be the next Mariano Rivera, a true closer."

"And what about that pretty young woman of yours, Cynthia?" I ask.

"Nineteen years in September," Vinnie says, bragging.

I whistle at the thought that a man can be married for nineteen years and still have a smile on his face when his wife is mentioned, like how Vinnie is smiling at me now.

"What can I say? Momma takes care of me."

"Nothing wrong with that," I reply.

"Are you here for Pastor Gutierrez?" Vinnie asks.

"Actually, I'm here for you."

"So what do you need, Nic? You wouldn't be here to see me if you didn't."

I have very few contacts in Miami. Of course, when you have a contact like Vinnie, you don't really need a lot of contacts. Vinnie is the church janitor, and he runs his own janitorial business. To meet Vinnie is to automatically like him and to want to do things for him. Vinnie has used his God-given charm to influence some high-powered people, and as a result, he's able to cash in and can get access to everything from opera seats to political fundraisers, even Miami Heat tickets.

"Douglas Madison. I need to get close to him."

"How close?"

"Close enough to wipe the lint off his suit jacket."

Vinnie lets out a whistle. "I don't know, Nic. You overestimate the influence I really have."

I know I put in for a large order, but my plan hinges on being able to apply pressure to dear old Douglas Madison.

"Come on, Vinnie. Impossible is not in your dictionary."

"No, but improbable is, and from where I'm standing, that's where we are," he says.

"There has to be someone you know that can get me close to Douglas Madison."

"And if I know that someone, what will you do for me?"

"Name it."

A sinister smile comes to Vinnie's face. He knows that a blank check from me is golden. I also see firsthand why Vinnie has managed to thrive for all of these years.

"This summer, we're taking the kids out to California. I want passes to Disneyland, both parks," Vinnie says.

A blank check from me and all Vinnie wants to do is hang out with Mickey Mouse? God bless him.

"I'll tell you what, I'll put you and the family up at the Disneyland Hotel as well."

"Deal." Vinnie extends his hand out to mine, and I shake it.

Vinnie puts his hands over his mouth and tosses around an idea. There has to be someone that can connect with Madison.

"Now that I think about it, I know a guy who used to work for me until he branched out on his own. He has a contract for a building that's owned by Knott's VP. I'll call him up."

"Vinnie, I need this to go down ASAP. I'm working with a small timetable."

"The way you sound, you make it seem like this man is a terrorist."

No, but his post is a financial terrorist. "No, nothing like that, but I'm only in town for a few days, two at the most. I need to meet up with him soon."

Vinnie gives me a head nod to confirm that he understands the urgency of the matter. "I'll give him a call and see what I can set up."

I can't help but to shake Vinnie's hand again. The next man is better than nothing. Now I just need to contact my friend Paul and see what I can dig up on the VP.

Chapter Twenty-seven

It's a familiar scene for me, sitting in a hotel room, the Bible open, and a glass of Jack Daniels in my hand. It's a familiar scene except for one twist; I have yet to take a drink. The desire to drink is strong, and I can't blame it on the devil. I welcomed the craving, and I didn't need the devil's temptation. I do need the Lord's grace to restore me, however.

"Lord, you know I want to take a drink, but I don't want the guilt that comes with it. Lord, help me to pour out this drink. Jesus, I need you."

I get up and though the desire is strong, I walk over to the bathroom with the drink in my hand. I avoid looking down to keep from taking a sip before I pour the drink out. The lights are already on when I enter the bathroom. It's a bad habit I have, but since I have paid for the room, I don't feel the need to conserve electricity. I turn on the faucet, and I then pour out the glass of Jack down the sink. It's hypnotic watching the brown liquor and water mixing together as they go down the drain. I set the glass next to the sink and grab the bottle and proceed to conduct that same experiment again. Now that I have eliminated the temptation in my room, I can refocus my attention on reading my Bible.

The book of Proverbs is known as a book of wisdom. For a foolish man such as myself, I find Proverbs to be a guide to a better path. I am seeking a better path. The last week is evident that if I continue down my current path, then I'm heading to cold, lonely, bitter grave. I turn to Proverbs 3:24:

When you lie down, you will not be afraid; when you lie down, your sleep will be sweet.

I lie down, but when I close my eyes, the image is not sweet. It's an image of Cameron's gun pointed at my face. I may have dodged the bullet in the physical realm, but mentally, I see the gun and this time, Adele is not standing behind Cameron with a shotgun. This time, it's lights out and a cold chill before I fade to black.

What's even more alarming than the image of being shot is that there is a part of me that wishes it all would've ended.

So many people fear death, but death doesn't scare me as much as most people. When I think of death, I think of an end to suffering. Victory represented more than a potential romance, but a chance for life and happiness and to not allow my demons of the past to devour me. Maybe I had too high of expectations of Victory. She's not my Savior; there's only one.

My phone alerts me that I have a new message. It takes me a moment, but I get up and walk over to the table to check my message. I see that it's actually an e-mail from Paul. The subject line of the e-mail reads, I got something good. I click on the link, and it takes me to the information that Paul uncovered. Something weird starts to happen as I scan over the little bit of information I can read from my smart phone. Something strange is happening to my face. Then it dawns on me: I'm smiling. I'm smiling at the fact that I just found my way to squeeze Douglas Madison and thus, cripple Randall Knott.

I stand across the street from Knott's Corporation Miami office, waiting for Miguel to give me the sign that the coast is clear. After I got the e-mail from Paul, I went and printed out the material. A few hours later, I get a call from Vinnie, letting me know that he has made good on his promise. So here I am outside, waiting for a way in.

There is one security guard working the front desk. I hope that he's not a problem. Moments later, Miguel shows up with and talks with the guard. Of course, I can't hear what they are saying, but they exchange a few laughs. Then the security guard gets up and leaves his post.

Once Miguel confirms that the coast is clear, he then signals for me to come on. I start to jog across the street dodging traffic. When I get across the street, he opens the door.

"Hurry, we only have a few minutes."

"What did you say to him?"

"That my wife made her famous chicken enchiladas and all he has to do is warm them up in the microwave."

Miguel walks me over to the elevator and uses his keycard.

"Text me when you're ready to come down."

I don't know what Vinnie did to put Miguel in debt to him where he would take such a huge risk, but I'm glad he did it.

I hop on the elevator and go up to the twelfth floor. I don't know if this plan will work, but it's worth a try. I get off the elevator and turn right. At the end of the hallway is an office with classical music playing. I walk up to the door and knock. I hear a little rumbling around until the door opens, and sure enough, Douglas Madison is on the other side.

"Can I help you?"

"Douglas Madison, my name is Nicodemus Dungy, and I have an important matter to discuss with you."

"I'm sorry, but I'm very busy." Douglas tries to close the door, but I put my foot in the way. "Listen, Mr. Madison,

I know you're very busy, but a few minutes of your time would be worth it because if I have to come back, then I'm returning with federal agents."

If he's a straitlaced guy like I think he is, then the mere threat of involving the police will be enough. If not, then I've just blown a golden opportunity to blindside Knott.

"Come in." Douglas opens the door, and I close it behind me.

"What's this all about Mr. . . . .?"

"Dungy, Nic Dungy."

I reach into my inside pocket and produce photos of the people murdered on the island. I drop them right in front of his desk.

"What's this?"

"These are the people your boss murdered."

"That's preposterous."

Denial can be deadly. I choose to show Douglas the photos first so that I can get his attention and throw him off balance.

"I don't know who you think you are, but you can't come in here and toss these photos on my desk and make allegations about my employer."

"I can, and I did. Now, I've told you my name, but that's not what's important. What's important is why I'm here to see you and the police are not here yet," I say.

"Speaking of police, how did you get in here?" Douglas tries to pick up the phone to call security.

I stop Douglas from dialing by taking the phone from him. This situation can get out of hand real fast, so for the sake of not ruining any more lives, it's time for me to explain why I'm here.

"Before you call the security and I call the police, I think you may want to give me two minutes to explain why I'm here," I say.

Douglas stops trying to take the phone from me and instead takes a seat in his chair. "Two minutes."

I start to pace the office. I see all of these awards and accolades Madison has collected over the years. What's even more impressive is he has an equal number of family photos and keepsakes. This is a man who gets what life's about. He understands that life is not a huge Monopoly board where one tries to obtain as much property and materials as possible. I can see that Madison's efforts and gains are for those who he holds dear, his true treasures, and his family.

"A minute and a half," Douglas says.

I lose my train of thought. So much has transpired that I don't where to start. I guess the best place would be with the information that is relevant to him and his current position.

"You are aware that Randall Knott likes to spend a lot of time in the Bahamas," I say.

"Yes, I know; what of it?"

"He also has a lot of business dealings on the island."

"I know this. Again, what of it? You have sixty seconds."

"You know of all of Knott's business dealings in both Miami and the Bahamas, there is not one piece of paper he has signed," I say.

The way Douglas starts to rub his forehead, I can tell that the clock has stopped, and I now have both his attention and the time to lay out my case.

"I don't see what this has to do with me," Douglas says.

"That's the just the thing. *Your* name is on every piece of document from the property Knott has acquired in Crystal Cove." I point to the pictures that are still on Douglas's desk. "The police will look into their deaths, and there is a paper trail that leads back to you, which means that if Randall Knott is brought up on charges, he can point the figure at you, and *you* would be the one going to jail."

Madison starts to rub his forehead even harder. I just dropped off a heavy load, and right now, I'm sure Madison is replaying all of those documents that he just blindly signed and never gave them a second thought. This whole time, Douglas never knew he was sealing his own fate.

"The purchases of the properties in Crystal Cove are legitimate acquisitions. There was nothing illegally done on our part."

"You sure about that?" I ask, but I can tell that Douglas is unsure.

I reach into my jacket pocket and pull out the file I got from Paul. I toss it on top of the pictures. Douglas picks up the file and starts to read through it. The information Paul sent was raw material, but I highlighted some to show the connection between the purchases and the alleged crimes that are associated with the purchases. Douglas reads over the material a few times before he sits back in his chair and lets out a deep sigh.

"I know how the media paints Mr. Knott out to be a bully, but he is really a good guy; he's not a killer." Douglas pans over the file and pictures on his desk. "There's no way he could've done this."

"You're willing to risk your family on that?"

Douglas doesn't say anything; he just sits there and weighs his options. The businessman is at odds with the family man. Which one will win?

"What do you want me to do?" he asks.

"I need you to testify in court about all of the shady dealings Knott has been involved in," I reply.

Douglas starts shaking his head. Even with a mountain of evidence on his desk, he is still loyal to the man who has made him wealthy.

"I can get you protection," I say.

"I can't."

"You have to." I point to the picture of the dead bodies. The pictures are my closing argument.

"No, I can't. I can't put my family at risk. I won't. There has to be another way."

I put my hands in my pocket and shrug my shoulders. My best option is protection, but then I remember that this is the businessman in Douglas talking. The family man would take the deal and start over. The vice president in him wants to take over the throne after Knott has been dethroned.

"I can't do it, but there is someone else," Douglas says.

"Who?"

"Trevor Morgan."

"Who's that?"

"Trevor Morgan was one of Mr. Knott's accountants. He was a little off, and he found things that he shouldn't have found." Madison takes a deep breath. "Knott fired him and branded him crazy. Trevor went off the grid."

"Mr. Madison, with all due respect, I don't have time for any wild goose chases. I came to you with a deal of a lifetime. A chance to get ahead of this thing before it blows. If you're not interested, then I wish you the best of luck."

"No, I swear. He was an accountant for Mr. Knott. He was an ex-war vet, and he was going on and on about what Knott was up to. He was labeled crazy, and then fired. He went off the grid. He has *evidence* on Knott."

"If I can't find him, then I need for you to testify," I say.

"Knott will suspect me."

"There's no way Knott won't suspect you. You're putting your family in danger. Let me help you."

"I won't promise anything," Douglas says.

"Let me be the one to make promises."

I scan the room and see the sincerity prayer next to his daughter's picture. Douglas is not only a family man, but a man of faith. It's funny how all of our relationships come down to faith.

"Do me a favor, Mr. Madison."

"What's that?"

"Pray about it. Let God lead you to the truth."

Madison just gives me a head nod, and that's all I need. I text Miguel to let him know I'm ready to come down. Now, it's all about finding Randall Knott's former accountant and get protection for him.

Chapter Twenty-eight

I track down Trevor Morgan to his ex-wife Cecile. The couple divorced shortly after Trevor was declared insane. Cecile retained her married name which says something about the affection she still has for her husband. It's actually a heartbreaking tale. Based on the information I gathered from the articles and medical records, the move is a result of Cecile not being able to pay for Trevor's medical bills. When Trevor lost his job, he also lost his family, and if there is some way I can help right this wrong, then that's what I will do.

Cecile lives in Dade County, a more urban-populated area of Miami. Christmas is in a few days, so most houses have their Christmas decorations put up. I also see that there are police cars parked in the driveway. Miami likes to maintain a strong police presence in its neighborhoods. Cecile's neighborhood has a lot of grass areas instead of sidewalks, so I park along the side of her house.

As I walk up to her doorstep I realize that it's amazing that she still maintains her home in the aftermath of her husband's demise. I ring the doorbell and moments later, Cecile opens the door. I can tell that she used to be more attractive but the years and stress of Trevor's plight has taken its toll on her.

"Can I help you?" Cecile asks.

"Hello, Mrs. Morgan. My name is Minister Nicodemus Dungy, and I'm here to talk to you about your husband."

Cecile tries to close the door. "I haven't seen or heard from Trevor in years."

I put my foot in the doorway. This is an aggressive move, but I need Mrs. Morgan to let me in and not shut me out. "Please, Mrs. Morgan, I know your family has been through a horrific ordeal, but I'm here to help."

"No one comes here to help. They just come to pry into my personal life with Trevor. I'm tired, and I just want to be left alone. Good day." She tries to close the door again.

"I know he's innocent," I say.

Cecile stops trying to close the door on me. She just stands with the door open and looks me in the eyes. I guess she's searching to see if my intentions are true.

"You can come in for a minute." She opens the door for me to enter.

I follow Cecile into the house and have a seat on the couch. She takes a seat on the love seat diagonal from me.

"There have been lawyers, activists, and others who have come by saying they can help. Then after awhile, they stop returning my phone calls and e-mails. Randall Knott's money and influence runs long, so forgive me for saying, but I don't think a minister can do anything different."

"I know all you've gotten over the years is a lot of broken promises, but I believe that I can expose Knott for the monster that he is, but I'll need your husband's help in doing so."

"Like I've said, I haven't seen Trevor in years. After he was publically scorned, he couldn't handle his family being ridiculed on account of him trying to do the right thing."

Cecile buries her face in her hands. I quickly scan the room for clues. The outside world may have labeled Trevor a crazy man who fabricated false information about a wealthy businessman, but in this home, Trevor's legacy as a father and a husband is still intact. His wedding photos and picture with his daughter, Peyton, decorated the walls and counters.

"My husband may be many things, but he's not a liar. If he said that Randall Knott embezzled money, then Randall Knott embezzled money. They destroyed my family to cover up a liar. What do I tell our daughter? Huh? What do I tell her about her father?"

"Was there anything about your husband that was different?"

"You know the war really did a number on my husband, but he wasn't crazy. I believe everything he said Randall Knott was up to was true."

The look on Cecile's face is not of a woman that is glad to be divorced and away from her crazy husband. Her look is of a woman who wishes her family could be made whole.

"Mommy, Mommy, Mommy, my doll is missing." Peyton, Trevor and Cecile's daughter, comes running in.

Peyton hops on her mother's lap. She has a birthday in April where she will turn five years old. A little girl shouldn't be without her father at such a young age. Peyton looks at me and doesn't say anything. She just waves at me. I wave back at her. This simple gesture feels both awkward and distant.

"I'll be right back." Cecile takes Peyton off her lap and gets up. She follows Peyton to her room.

"Lord, forgive me." As soon as Cecile is out of sight, I start looking for clues.

I can't go into any of the rooms, so I have to find something in the living room that will help me find the location of Trevor. I come across a stack of bills and decide to rifle through them quickly. They have not all been already opened, which means that this is today's mail. There is a storage bill and in it, it showed a paid balance. I also notice that it is a large storage unit. A single mother with one child wouldn't need a big storage unit, and that may just be the clue that I need. I put the mail back and head toward the door right before Cecile returns. I may have found Trevor and the leverage I need to bring Knott down.

From Mrs. Morgan's house, I drive over to Dade County Public Storage. I saw the storage number on the bill, and I plan to take a peek into that storage unit. I'm not sure what I'll find, but I have to follow all leads, even if the leads are a dead end.

I pull up to the two-story Dade County Public Storage building. The main office is closed and only the security lights are on. I pull into the visitor parking spot and turn off the car. I know what storage number I need to go to, but I don't have a clue how to get into the building. I step out of the car and walk up to the security gate. I could try to climb it, but being in a suit with dress shoes might make my attempts embarrassing, to say the least.

A flashlight starts to move, and my entrance to the building may be arriving soon.

"We're closed," a security guard says.

The guard's skin is almost as bright as his flashlight. In fact, I don't even think he needs a flashlight to carry around.

"I know, but it's really important. I left my key in my storage unit."

"You're going to have to come back tomorrow," the guard says.

"Listen, buddy, it can't wait." I motion for the officer to look down. He spots a Ben Franklin in my hands.

"You need to be quick," the guard says.

"I will and thank you."

It's wrong to bribe, but I feel like the bigger crime is how many hardworking people in this country are grossly underpaid. I enter the building and press the code I found on the bill. The elevator opens. I enter and press the second floor. In truth, I've seen maybe one too many scary movies. I start to get a real eerie feeling being in a storage building with only myself and a security guard on site. I could be murdered, and no one would hear me scream since the security officer is patrolling outside.

I get off at the second floor. There's a lot of darkness between the two security lights that occupy each floor. I follow the aisle that's closer to storage 297. As I get closer to the storage unit number, I see that the light is on. I walk to the outside of the unit and take a look inside. This storage unit is a miniapartment. There is a chair and small desk with plenty of newspaper clippings and books. A cup of coffee sits next to the desk with steam rising . . . Which means that someone is here and left. Perhaps the sound from my shoes scared off the occupant, but I believe I have found Trevor Martin.

Suddenly, I feel an arm slip around my throat and squeeze. I try to fight my assailant off, but my attempts are futile. Soon I'll lose consciousness. I stump on my assailant's foot with my feet, and I throw an elbow to the midsection.

"Trevor Martin?" I struggle to say.

"Who are you? How did you find me?"

"I'm here to help. I know the truth about Randall Knott. I know what he did, and I want to bring him down."

It took everything within me explain myself, but my assailant finally loosened his grip, and I was able to breathe again. It took a moment to clear my throat, but when I turned around, there is Trevor Martin standing in front of me. In his pictures, Trevor doesn't have a beard, but he has since grown one. His hair is longer, and there is an odor about him. At the same time, I can tell that he tries to cover up his lack of being able to take a shower with cologne and deodorant.

"You're crazy if you think you can take down Knott," Trevor says.

There's the pot calling the kettle black. Trevor is practically living like the Unabomber and not even the glimmer of hope for redemption can move him.

"Knott tried to have me killed, and he destroyed your career and your family. I don't know about you, but I'm not about to let that slide."

Trevor starts to laugh. He must think I'm crazy; again, the feeling is mutual.

"You're dreaming; you can't take down Knott. He has too many angles."

"No man walking this earth is untouchable. He won't see me coming, but I need your help."

"Forget about it. I lost everything chasing after him. The only reason why I'm alive right now is because I knew how to take a whipping and walk away. I walked away from my family, and that was the best thing to do."

"I met your wife and your daughter. I know she still loves you, and if there is any chance of you being reunited as a family, you'll need my help."

"You can't bring down someone like Knott and be able to live peacefully."

"I can provide you with protection."

"Boy, you really are flying in the dark now, aren't you? If you knew the truth about Knott, you would rent a storage unit right next to mine," he says.

I have to be willing to see this thing to its conclusion. Trevor has amassed a lot of information, and there's no doubt that there are a lot more people who stand to lose if the truth about Knott is let out.

Trevor starts to point at the different news clippings and different color strings that shows the connection. It's fascinating, and it tells a dark narrative of one of the wealthiest men on the planet, but I need for Trevor to make sense of his findings.

"Political corruption from the last three elections; why do you think the same party gets reelected? Why do you think there's such a low turnout of the minority vote in Dade County? Knott makes sure that we can't vote, and that the only people who go into office are those who serve Knott's best interests," Trevor says.

"But Obama won the last two elections," I reply.

Trevor chuckles and gives me a dismissive wave. I hope he's not about to go on an Illuminati rant.

"It don't matter who sits in the White House. Knott cares about who runs the state, and that's where he focuses his influence."

Trevor walks over to other news clippings that, at a glance, seem unrelated. They are clippings of murders that are suspected mob hits and clippings from articles about megachurches.

"Mob money, church money—he scams them all into thinking that they are investing with Randall Knott. In truth, Knott is a master of building with other people's money. He cheats them out of their investments."

"How?" I ask.

"I was cooking his books. He fabricates false figures and gets people to invest more money than is necessary. He likes to use the mob and churches and community outreach programs, because they'll never do the due diligence necessary to find out about their investments."

Trevor shakes his head, and the picture that he's trying to paint is starting to come into view.

"You discovered this, and he fired you?" I ask.

"I discovered that this man has offshore accounts, dummy corporations, insider trading. He's just never been caught."

"Well, that's about to change. Listen, Trevor, you don't deserve to spend the rest of your life hiding. Let me use the information you gathered to expose Knott, and I'll give you protection."

Trevor starts to shake his head as he walks around his small space and looks at his life's work. "I want you to guarantee that you will find protection for me."

I hate making promises, especially when there are so many moving pieces, but what kind of man would I be if I didn't take the leap of faith. "I promise."

Trevor hesitates before he goes into his filing cabinet and pulls out a file that is at least two inches thick. He hands me the file.

"Let's see what you can do. I can't give you everything yet, but that's at least enough to get the ball rolling with Witness Protection."

I open the file and thumb through it. Extortion, racke-teering, bribery—you name it. I have Randall Knott cold, and that's only a sample of what Trevor has on Knott. "Is this your only copy?"

"Of course not, there are others, but I won't tell you where."

Fair enough. Trevor gave me what I need, and now all I need to do is provide him with protection, and I know who to contact for that.

Chapter Twenty-nine

I flew back to California on a red-eye flight from Miami. I can't even begin to describe the level of exhaustion that I feel right now, but before I can rest I have to finish what I started with Knott. I pick my car up from the long-term parking lot and head straight to my destination.

I don't have time to call anyone up, not even my two closest friends, Garland and Paul. I don't even have time to stop by my place in Carson and check the mail. I have a very short window of opportunity to bring Knott down, and I can't miss it. Knott doesn't make a lot of mistakes, and if I don't catch him now, then I won't get another opportunity.

Driving along the 405, I have to admit that I miss home. I miss the island too, but since I almost didn't make it back from the island, I prefer the congestion of a big city to the beauty of a small island. At least that's the way I feel now.

It's four a.m., and I am heading to Johnny's Donuts in Gardena. This is a spot where I'm a silent partner. I went to high school with Johnny, and we maintained contact since our high school graduation. A few years back, Johnny found himself in trouble with his business and needed some cash. Since I didn't want to see a longtime friend lose his dream, I decided to help him out. In return, I get unlimited bear claws and privileges to use his office to conduct meetings that I don't want people to know about.

I pull into the parking spot, and all I see is Johnny's van parked outside. That means the person whom I'm supposed to meet hasn't arrived yet. I get out of the car and go inside. Johnny sees me and grabs a bear claw and hands it to me.

"Thank you, sir," I say.

"No problem, Nic."

John turns around and grabs a Styrofoam cup and pours. He knows just how I like my coffee: French Vanilla cream and two sugars.

"The Lakers lost last night," he says.

"I heard. That's starting to become a regular occurrence."

"Yeah, they need trades and a new coach." He hands me the coffee.

"Gracias. I'm going to go in the back, and when my friend arrives, just tell her to meet me in the back," I say.

"I got you."

I walk into Johnny's office and remove the stack of newspapers in his chair which I place on his desk. I'm glad the actual donut shop is not a reflection of Johnny's office. Just when I'm getting comfortable eating my donut and drinking my coffee, in walks Special Agent Kim West with a Muslim shawl wrapped around her head. Kim can't be any taller than five feet two, with a mocha complexion and almond-shaped eyes.

"You picked a great time to cash in on your favor. I'm risking having my cover blown for you," she says. Kim gives me a stern look. I did take an inopportune time to cash in on a favor, but it's necessary.

"I know, but this couldn't wait."

"Is it a matter of national security?" she asks.

"Not exactly."

"Well, then, it could wait. The only reason why I'm here is because I'm a woman of my word and the text message suggests that you're in trouble," Kim says.

"I wasn't aware that I was," I say.

Kim rolls her eyes. We have very few things in common—but one of those things is hating when people insult our intelligence.

"You sent a text in all lower case. You *never* send texts in lower case unless you are in a rush, which suggests anxiety. You also misspelled the word *urgent* which you never do. In fact, you never use the word *urgent* in your texts. You spelled *need* with an extra *'e,'* and you sent me two follow-up texts within twenty minutes of each other. Don't play with me." Kim bats her eyes at me.

I don't know what division Kim works for in the FBI, but given her sharp analytical abilities, I think it's safe to say that she's a criminal profiler. At the same time, she's undercover, and I can't tell what she does, but I know one thing: I hate being beholden to anyone.

"Funny, I don't recall me saying it could wait or giving you a hard time when you needed me to get your brother into seminary," I say.

For all of my skills in the dark arts of being a fixer, I do have one skill that stands on the right side of the light. I have tremendous pull with faculties throughout the country. Kim's brother wanted to attend Full Gospel Seminary, a prominent school located out in Dallas, and I got him in. Of course, for the last three years, Kim has owed me a favor that I never cashed in on until today. It's not every day a federal agent is in debt to me, so I know that I can't waste a favor on something frivolous.

"Seriously? You're going to threaten a woman with a glock pistol strapped to her? Do you know I can make one phone call to my buddies in the NSA and have you put on a no-fly list? Don't play with me, Nic. Now what do you need?"

Brilliant, sexy, and feisty, Kim is the ideal woman for me if it weren't for her profession and the fact that she does keep her gun on her at all times. I'm also afraid she would dig up stuff about my past I would rather keep hidden.

"I have a family that I will need witness protection for, and I need you to get ahold of your contacts at the marshals' office."

"Hold up." Kim puts her hands up. "I'm going to stop you right there. I owe you a favor, not the U.S. Marshal. The marshals are not at your disposal, and I'm not just going to contact the marshals' office. I need a reason."

"I'm about to hand Randall Knott's head on a silver platter to your people, but before I do that, I need WIT-SEC in place for this family."

"Randall Knott . . . the billionaire?" Kim asks.

I give her a head nod, and we both know a billionaire has the resources to make someone disappear instantly. Even government protection is no guarantee of safety, but I have to provide Trevor and his family with some kind of protection.

The look on Kim's face suggests that I gave her a good enough reason. She bats her eyes at me, then extends her hand as a gesture for me to show her what I have on Knott. I hand her the file Trevor gave me. Kim starts to scan the file, and her eyes widen at the sight of the information contained within the file.

"How credible is your source?" Kim asks.

"He's been discredited," I say.

"You sure it's legitimate?"

"It is."

"If you're wrong about Knott he's going to set fire to everything and everyone you touch."

"Must you be so cynical?" I ask.

"I only take Christ for His word. The list ends there," she says.

"It's a legit source," I say.

"You sure *you* won't need WITSEC?" Kim asks.

"I can take care of myself, but my friend needs a clean slate for his wife, his daughter, and himself."

Kim scans over the documents again before she closes the file and hands it back to me. "No promises. I'll see what I can do."

"Thank you."

"This is a pretty big favor, so *you're* going to owe *me*."

"I got you. If you ever need to get away somewhere and relax, I know a place in the Bahamas, and I know a lady with a beautiful spot to rent."

"I'll keep that in mind." Kim folds her arms. I guess she's not sure what to do next. "Listen, Nic, I have to be back before sunrise."

"What are you up to?" I ask.

"None of your business. I mean, stay in your lane. You do you, and I'm going to do me."

Kim heads out the door, but stops to look back at me. "Be careful, Nic."

"You too."

We both told each other to be careful, but the truth is, both Kim and I have a knack for running into danger instead of running from it.

***

A Gulfstream 650 jet is like having a portable condominium. Randall Knott decorated the interior of the plane in an egg-shell white. I was enjoying a drink and watching CNN when Randall Knott walks on board.

"I wasn't aware that I had an extra passenger," Knott says.

"So where are you headed, Knott? Dubai? Hong Kong, or somewhere else where there's no extradition?"

"Listen, Nic, I know we haven't had a chance to hash out the details surrounding the casino and your involvement, but I promise you that we'll work it out as soon as I get back."

"I'm not worried about it because there's not going to be a casino deal. In fact, your schedule is going to be pretty open for the next few decades."

"Listen, I don't know what you're talking about, but I don't appreciate you coming onto my plane unannounced."

I take a sip of the drink. I love having a self-proclaimed master of the universe by the stones. "You have very expensive taste when it comes to Hennessey, Mr. Knott. Beauté du Siècle. That has to set you back, what, a hundred grand?"

"Get off my plane right now!" Knott says.

"This is the same liquor you had Cameron deliver to his brother Demetrius. Only that bottle was laced with poison," I say before I pour the glass out on the carpet.

"What the—" Knott advances toward me, but I stand up, and he realizes that while he may have more money than me, he'll lose in a hand-to-hand fight.

"I'm calling the police."

"You don't get it, do you? Where's your pilot? Where's the flight attendant?" I ask.

"What are you talking about?" Knott is befuddled.

"Take a look outside of the window."

Knott follows my instructions and looks outside his window. FBI agents scramble outside of his plane.

"The feds gave me the honor of telling you that you're going to spend the rest of your life in prison. Extortion, racketeering—you name it, but you and I both know that there is another jacket you deserve to wear—murderer."

"Murderer?" Knott says.

"You used Cameron to do your dirty work, and he killed three people and tried to kill me."

"You could've come to me, and we could've worked something out," Knott says.

"As you can see, this is not something that you can just cut the check for and it's over and done with," I say.

Knott looks at me, and then he looks outside the window. Agents are now outside of their cars positioned to take him down as soon as he steps off the plane. He starts to laugh.

"Hot darn, boy, you're good. Naïve, though. I won't spend a day in prison, and if I do, it'll be better than the slum you live in."

"Even if you buy your way out of prison, you still won't escape God and His laws."

Knott gives me a dismissive wave as he heads toward the door. "You better hope that God protects you, because you had a brilliant opening move, Nic, but I will get the checkmate. Just you wait and see."

Knott walks out of his plane like he's a politician greeting his loyal constituents. As soon as he touches the ground, the feds move in and arrest him. Knott has a smile on his face the whole time, as if he knew a punch line to a joke we haven't heard. I have a seat and pour a glass of this very fine Hennessey. I'm quitting after this drink. I'm going to sober up and this isn't a bad way to go before I go back on the wagon.

Chapter Thirty

Three days later, I get a text from Paul who I delivered Trevor's file to. I click on the link, and there is Paul's article showing a shamed Randall Knott in handcuffs. He will be charged for extortion and racketeering. He should be charged for murder as well, but there wasn't enough to make that charge stick. It doesn't matter though, the Lord will return before Randall Knott gets out of prison. Justice served in some form is better than no justice at all.

I've been back in L.A. for a week, and I wish I was back at the island. I didn't miss the traffic, and I'm ready to go crazy sitting on the 105 freeway. It's two o'clock in the afternoon, and it's still bumper-to-bumper traffic. What is even more frustrating is my exit is the next exit. I have to go to the Forum to meet up with Pastor Bryant. He's in town for a conference, and we have some unfinished business to settle.

I pull into a front parking space and walk up the steps to the entrance. I remember coming to the Forum for years and going to the Laker games. This place is a landmark, but over the years, it has lost its luster. Pastor Bryant meets me on the steps.

"I should start calling you the Formidable Nic Dungy," Pastor Bryant says.

I still respect Pastor Bryant, but after today, I wouldn't be sad if I didn't see him again until the Rapture. Bryant removes an envelope from his coat pocket and hands it to me.

"As promised," he says.

I open the envelope and see that it's a check for $1.5 million.

"This is more than I expected."

"That's because I need you to do one more thing, but when I tell you, I believe you will want to do it for free."

"You have *got* to be kidding me," I say.

Pastor Bryant is not taken aback by my response. He knows what I've been through and that he doesn't have the right to ask any more of me. I don't care how many zeros he puts on the check.

"Randall Knott is not the only guilty party in this. There are others," he says.

This is the part in the story where the hero takes the $1.5 million-dollar check, rips it up, and throws it into Pastor Bryant's face . . . but I'm not a hero. I put that check in my pocket because I've earned it.

"You mean your friends from the Cloth? What happened? Were they not radical enough for you?"

Bryant purses his lips. I know that his involvement in the Cloth is a sensitive issue.

"Cole went to them after he met with the witch doctor. He told them that he was out. He felt like he should've left a long time ago. He knew what Knott was up to, and he didn't want any part of it. He tried to reason with the rest of us, but we weren't having it."

Pastor Cole wasn't as lucky as Bryant. He didn't even get the chance to be free from the Cloth. Bryant is enjoying a freedom that should've been Pastor Cole's as well.

"This isn't a simple request," I say.

"Hence, the reason for the extra money," Bryant says.

"I don't think you understand the gravity of what you're asking me. If I pull back the veil, then the church is going to suffer. Do you realize that's going to shine a spotlight on all of your ministries?"

Pastor Bryant leans in closer to me with his hands clasped together in prayer. "These men called Cole their brother, their leader. When he was found dead, whatever suspicions they had, they swept them under a rug. I don't care if it gives the church a black eye. The church will survive and thrive so long as Christ is lifted up; it will draw men to Him."

If Christ be lifted up, I will draw all men. I don't know where or when this concept got lost, but it's time to rediscover it. Maybe the church community can be rebuilt by following these profound words of the Gospel.

"What do you need me to do?"

"Bring them down. They're all here in L.A. They have even rented a suite in Hollywood," Pastor Bryant says.

I normally don't play in my own backyard because there is too much of a blowback if things goes south, but the Cloth being in L.A. is too good to pass up. I also have the home court advantage, and I can use my wide range of contacts.

"I'll see what I can do," I say.

"I have faith that you'll do your level best."

I walk away and head to the car with a $1.5 million-dollar check in my possession and a chance to bring a powerful organization down. First, I'm going to stop by the bank.

Later on that night, I find myself outside the Grand Hotel in Hollywood. While it's not the most luxurious spot, compared to the W Hotel and other prominent spots, the Grand Hotel does have a rich history. Back in the day, names like Frank Sinatra, Doris Day, and Steve McQueen used to frequent this hotel. Nowadays, it just stands out like a relic from the past in an otherwise, fast-paced modern era.

I pull into the parking lot behind the hotel. The parking lot may not be full, but the fleet of cars outside tells the story of what type of guests occupy the Grand Hotel. Ferraris, Bentleys, Maseratis and Range Rovers, a Mercedes and Lexus in this parking lot seem like average cars. In fact, I'm afraid that my BMW doesn't pass the luxury test.

According to Bryant, whenever the Cloth is in town, they would rent two extended SUVs and drive up to this very hotel. Near the back exit are two black SUVs. They are here, and they have the trucks positioned so that they can leave at a moment's notice. I grab a phone and send a quick text to my friend.

> Be here in 10 minutes
> Nic

After I press SEND, I send one more text message to my source on the inside. Then I get out of the car and head toward the back exit. The clock is ticking, and it's a gamble if these guys are not doing anything but reading the Bible or praying or playing cards. My source from inside the hotel comes out of the back exit.

Mike Austin is a young man that used to attend the church that I was a minister at before I went into the problem-solving business. I actually helped him get a job at the Westin Hotel in downtown Long Beach. He worked there for a few years until he applied for a position as a concierge at the Grand Hotel.

Tall and handsome, he has grown into a fine young man and a vital source to tearing down this organization. I love having the home court advantage.

"Good to see you, Mr. Dungy," Mike says.

"Hey, Mike, how's your mom?"

"God is good. Her cancer is in remission."

"I'll be praying for her," I say.

I reach into my pocket and peel out three one hundred-dollar bills and hand them to Mike who flashes a Kool-Aid smile.

"Thanks, Mr. Dungy." Mike examines the money before he puts it in his pocket.

"The extra hundred is for your mother. Get her some flowers for me."

"Will do." Mike hands me a room key. "They're in the penthouse suite."

"I appreciate this, Mike. Now go on back to your shift. There is going to be some fireworks, but not to worry. This city loves scandals, and the number of guests that come to your hotel as a result of this scandal will likely triple."

Mike gives me a head nod and shows me the way to the elevator. I walk into the hotel through the back entrance and pass through the kitchen on my way to the service elevator.

No one seems to notice me. I step inside and press the letter *P* for the penthouse and use the special key to close the elevator door and have it take me up to the top floor.

My mind races through a hundred different scenarios, and none of them have a happy ending. This present trial and tribulation has caused me to lose faith in a favorable outcome, among other things. I arrive at the penthouse floor and step off the elevator. At the end of the hall is a security guard outside of the door. I didn't expect to see a guard; I didn't plan to encounter one either. I walk toward the door and try to think up a plan to get inside. I have to get inside in order for my plan to work.

"Boy, it's is difficult to find this place," I say to the guard.

"Who are you?" the guard asks.

"Who am I? Are you *kidding* me? I'm Minister Nicodemus Dungy, and I'm here for the party. Why else would I be here?"

"I'm not supposed to let anyone in."

"Of course not. You're not supposed to let anyone in that's *not* about the Cloth's business."

The guard's eyes enlarged. I can tell he's turning over in his mind that if I'm not a member of the Cloth, then how do I know about them and why am I here?

"You got a name, slick?" I ask.

"Kent."

"Are we taking care of you? I mean, are we paying you well?"

Kent shrugs his shoulders. "Y'all paying me all right."

That's all I need to hear. I reach into my pocket and pull out two one hundred-dollar bills. I fold them and extend them out to Kent. "A little extra something for you and we put this whole thing behind us."

Kent hesitates before he takes the money, then he opens the door. I walk in, and this time, I'm not surprised to see drinking, smoking, and naked girls being chased around by so-called men of God. I slam the door shut, and get their attention. Pastor Jackson is sitting down smoking a cigar with a half-naked Asian girl on his lap.

"What do you want, Nic?" Pastor Jackson asks.

"I just want to simply bring that which is dark to the light."

The men start laughing. I'm sure that they think they are above the law and that they have God in their back pocket.

"Last I checked, you weren't invited to this party," another pastor says.

"I guess you haven't heard the news. Randall Knott was arrested this morning and charged, so your casino adventure is on hold for at least the next forty years."

"What do we care for? We didn't cut him a check. There'll be other opportunities," Jackson says.

"It doesn't bother you one bit that Cole lost his life dealing with Knott?"

"It was Cole's idea to deal with Knott. You can't dance with the devil and expect to lead," Jackson says.

The men start laughing again, and I'm getting that sour taste in my mouth that proceeds throwing up.

"Now don't let the door hit you where the good Lord split you," Jackson says.

The men enjoy their laugh, and I get a text telling me that my friend is outside.

"Enjoy the laugh, because like I said, I'm here to let in the light." I walk over and open the door.

A cameraman comes bursting in, taking photos, with my friend Paul trying to get past Kent. The pastors and girls try to scramble and hide. I walk over to Kent, who has Paul in a full nelson and put my hand on his shoulder.

"The police are on their way. Leave now or go to jail," I say.

It takes only a moment for Kent to realize what I am telling him, then he releases Paul and disappears. After Paul shakes off Kent's assault, he then walks into the room.

"Now, *this* is my kind of party," Paul says as the shameful pastors still try to run and hide. "Don't worry, gentlemen, we have all of your pictures, and they will be in the paper tomorrow morning, but that's the *least* of your problems."

Paul is right, that is the least of their worries. I gave Paul the order to call the police just as soon as he met up with Mike and got the penthouse key. The Cloth is going down for embezzlement, among other things.

"Big mistake, Nic," Jackson says to me from the other side of the room. "Big mistake!"

He may be right. It's a mistake to set fire to my profession and expose a dirty, dark secret within the church. It is a mistake, but for now . . . It feels *good*.

***

Hours later, with a slew of reporters at the scene, I have a cigarette and watch as members of the Cloth are packed away in police vans. Most of them have their heads down to cover up their image, except for Pastor Jackson. Pastor Jackson has his head held high. He does not feel shame for what he has done, and I don't know whether to applaud him for his conviction or to be repulsed by it. Paul emerges from the slew of reporters.

"Two great stories in one week. You're back on my Christmas list, my friend," he says with a grin.

"That's all I wanted for Christmas," I say.

"You know, they're going to crucify you. You're not going to be able to do what you do anymore now that they can't trust you."

"It doesn't matter, I'm thinking about retiring anyway."

"Really?" Paul asks.

I take a puff of my cigarette and let the smoke out. "I've seen too much, and I have done too much. I want my remaining days on this earth to be peaceful."

"Good luck with that," Paul says.

"I don't believe in luck. I believe in God's will."

"Well, since you're retired, I might as well buy you a burger down the street."

"That sounds like a good idea."

"I mean, it's not the best retirement party, but it's *something*," he says.

"It's more than enough."

Paul and I walk down the street looking at the names on the walk of fame and debate the merits of the recipients. I spend the evening with a friend laughing and joking, and for the first time, I don't feel the weight of being a fixer on my shoulders. I am no longer Minister Nic Dungy, church problem solver. I am Nicodemus Dungy, and I can be at peace with being nothing more than what God created me to be.

Epilogue

Flying high above, I realize it's been six months since I left Crystal Cove. I didn't expect to see the island anytime soon, and I'm sure glad that I am returning on better circumstances.

"We're getting ready to touch down, Doc," Donny says.

I look out ahead and see only clouds. Donny has been flying for so long that his instincts tell him when he is close to his destination. It's rare to see a smile on Donny's face, but it's understood considering that he's doing what he loves and that this is a special day.

I look outside the window and see the picturesque water and the outline of Crystal Cove. I have a smile on my face as if it's the first time I've seen the island. I didn't expect to be back so soon. I guess the events that transpired from my last visit brought the two closer together. I always felt like the phrase "Life is short" was relative. Life may appear to be short, but it feels a lot longer when a person is alone.

Donny lands the plane with precision, and I wonder what will happen to this airport. Demetrius is dead, and Randall Knott is in a federal prison. Knott confessed to everything and got a reduced sentence. That means this airport, which is a symbol of the power struggle between Knott and Demetrius, is now open to new ownership. I pray that the new owner, or owners, will see the predecessors' demise as a cautionary tale.

Epilogue

"We have to hurry. I'll drive you to my place, and we can change in time before it starts," Donny says as he ties down the plane.

I guess the greatest change aside from Sammy and Adele finding love is an improved relationship between Donny and his father. I am hopeful that there isn't a relationship above reconciliation. I hope for my own life that this is true. I haven't seen or heard from Victory since she left. I wanted to call her, but that didn't seem like the best way to apologize. I wanted to get on a plane and head to Sacramento and talk to her face to face, but I am too much of a coward. I'm not going to try to win her back. I just want to apologize to her and thank her for giving me a glimpse of what could've been; even something as simple as "I'm sorry" and "thank you" required too much courage on my part.

The area of the beach where I used to take my daily swims has been transformed into an outdoor chapel. About a dozen or so chairs are set up for an intimate ceremony where only close friends and family are invited. I consider myself fortunate that Adele and Sammy would want me present on their big day.

I stand next to Donny who is standing next to Sammy. The preacher is in position, and the guests have arrived.

"Boy, God is good. I didn't think I would find myself up here again," Sammy says.

"I meant to tell you, Mom says congratulations," Donny tells him.

"Make sure you tell her I said hello next time you talk with her," Sammy replies.

Sammy hired a local band to play music for the guests. They play island music which puts everyone in a festive mood. For a moment, the island is beautiful again, and I can let go of the fact that I almost died on this island.

The music changes, and everyone turns to see the bride coming. It's Adele's day, and she deserves to be the center of attention, but the person walking her down the aisle has *my* attention. Adele is being escorted by Victory. This is the first time I have seen Victory since she has left the island. Her eyes are locked onto me as well.

This moment couldn't be any more awkward, and at the same time, beautiful. Imagine a man and woman who have long denied their feelings for each other are getting married. Now imagine that Adele and Sammy's two witnesses are a couple that never really cultivated their relationship. That is the conundrum I have before me today. Adele has made a beautiful bride, and I am glad to see Sammy happy, but what I am really happy to see is that Victory made the trip. Victory is also beautiful in her signature sundress. Her eyes bounce back and forth from a tearful Adele to me. My eyes remain on her. I don't even pay attention to the minister's words. Victory glances at me through the corner of her eye and smiles. That smile, it always levels me.

"Adele, I've loved you since the day I first met you, and I can't think of a better way to cement our love then with God and all of our family and friends present and a song I would like to sing."

"Sammy, if you start singing, I'll leave you at the aisle," Adele says.

The whole crowd laughs. Even Sammy with his bruised pride lets out a laugh. It's clear that these two are determined to love each other and not change. The rest of the ceremony plays out like a traditional wedding ceremony.

"By the power invested in me, I now pronounce you man and wife," the preacher says.

Sammy and Adele and the crowd erupt. The newlyweds walk into their new lives hand in hand. Everyone starts to make their way toward Adele's house where the reception will be held. Everyone except for Victory, who stands at the shore and looks out at the ocean. This is my chance to set things right. I walk over to Victory and stand beside her.

"It was a beautiful ceremony," I say.

Victory looks over as the newlyweds help each other up the hill. "They look happy, and that's the main thing."

Where do I start? What can I say? The last word I heard from Victory was in the letter she left me. I still have that letter as a morbid reminder not to waste an opportunity to love someone special.

"Let me ask you something," Victory says.

"Shoot," I say.

"What happened in L.A. six months ago? Was that you?"

Victory must be referring to the night some of the most charismatic and renowned religious leaders got carted off in a van by the LAPD. Some in the church are heralding it as the black day in the modern church. I call it a good start to a much-needed reformation.

"It had to be done," I say.

"Did it?"

"I'm sorry. I'm sorry I kept you in the dark, but I couldn't fathom something happening to you on account of me," I tell her.

"So, who are you? Are you the person who either fixes things or destroys things in the name of God?"

"No. Not anymore. I'm just Nic. I'm going to do what I should've done years ago and let God work on the flawed men and women of the world, myself included."

Victory bites her bottom lip. She's mulling over something. I pray that it's something in my favor.

"Next time, you come and visit me," Victory says.

That's exactly what I want to hear. No relationship is beyond redemption, thank you Jesus.

"How about I take you on another trip? Just you and me," I suggest.

"How? You don't have a job."

I chuckle to myself. If she only knew. "I'll be able to manage it."

"Come on, we have a reception to attend. Let's not be rude." Victory extends her hand.

I walk with Victory up the hill toward Adele's house. Sammy and Adele are not the only ones starting a new chapter. I'm beginning to write a new chapter as well. My days as a church problem solver are a distant memory. From this day forth, I will put my energy toward my relationship with God, and I'll give Victory a fair shot. Who knows? Perhaps I wasn't meant to be alone after all.

Readers' Questions

1. Should Nic have kept the money Pastor Bryant paid him?
2. In this book, we encounter a secret religious group known as the Cloth. Do you believe that such a group exists?
3. One of the major themes throughout the novel dealt with God and the prosperity doctrine. Do you feel that this was an accurate assessment of churches who teach prosperity?
4. Was it easy figuring out the murderer?
5. Do you think there is a future for Nic and Victory?
6. What do you think is in the future for Sammy and Adele?
7. Do you think Nic Dungy will stay retired?
8. Which character would you like to see in another book?
9. Would you be interested in reading another Minister Nic Dungy story?
10. In this book, you are introduced to an FBI agent named Kim West. Are you curious to learn more about Ms. West?

AUTHOR'S BIO

Dijorn Moss was born and raised in Carson, California. He graduated from San Jose State University in 2003 with a degree in English. Dijorn currently lives in Long Beach, California, with his wife, Trinea, and their son, Caleb.

UC HIS GLORY BOOK CLUB!

www.uchisglorybookclub.net

UC His Glory Book Club is the spirit-inspired brain-child of Joylynn Ross, Author and Acquisitions Editor of Urban Christian, and Kendra Norman-Bellamy, Author for Urban Christian. This is an online book club that hosts authors of Urban Christian. We welcome as members all men and women who have a passion for reading Christian-based fiction.

UC His Glory Book Club pledges our commitment to provide support, positive feedback, encouragement, and a forum whereby members can openly discuss and review the literary works of Urban Christian authors.

There is no membership fee associated with UC His Glory Book Club; however, we do ask that you support the authors through purchasing, encouraging, providing book reviews, and of course, your prayers. We also ask that you respect our beliefs and follow the guidelines of the book club. We hope to receive your valuable input, opinions, and reviews that build up, rather than tear down our authors.

What We Believe:

—We believe that Jesus is the Christ, Son of the Living God.

—We believe the Bible is the true, living Word of God.

—We believe all Urban Christian authors should use their God-given writing abilities to honor God and share the message of the written word God has given to each of them uniquely.

—We believe in supporting Urban Christian authors in their literary endeavors by reading, purchasing and sharing their titles with our online community.

—We believe that in everything we do in our literary arena should be done in a manner that will lead to God being glorified and honored.

We look forward to the online fellowship with you. Please visit us often at www.uchisglorybookclub.net.

Many Blessing to You!
Shelia E. Lipsey,
President, UC His Glory Book Club